The Legends of King Arthur : Book 2

GAWAIN AND THE GREEN KNIGHT

Inspired by the medieval English poem

By Ben Gillman

This novel is entirely a work of fiction. Any resemblance to actual persons, living or dead, events or localities is entirely coincidental. Any reference to historical persons or characters are for the benefit of the narrative and is entirely for fictional purposes.

Editor: Nick Bowman

Cover Credit: Fiona Jayde Media

For Mom & Dad

who always supported my love of adventure

FOREWORD

"In heavy darkness drowsing he dream-words muttered,
as a man whose mind was bemused with many mournful
thoughts,
how destiny should his doom on that day bring him
when he at the Green Chapel the great man would meet,
and be obliged his blow to abide without debate at all."

-from the medieval English poem, "Sir Gawain and the Green
Knight"
Translated by J.R.R. Tolkien – 1925

TABLE OF CONTENTS

~ ~ ~

PROLOGUE
The Fall of the Bear King

When King Lot was only six months old, before he was actually a king at all, his parents gave him his very first teddy bear. And in just under two weeks, he had completely torn it to bits.

At first, his royal mother and father thought it was positively the cutest and most endearing thing they had ever seen. They were only too happy to replace the shredded bear with a new whole untarnished one. Lot reduced that one down to torn fabric and fluff in just under one week. His parents supplied another which only lasted five days. Then another. Which was gone overnight.

After that his parents tried to switch to more sturdy toys and presents. Lot was given carved horses, fairy-tale books and wooden swords, but they were all quickly tossed aside where they piled up in the corner barely touched. Instead the child howled and screamed to be given another stuffed bear. When his sleep-deprived, headache-addled parents finally conceded, Lot quickly ripped the bear to pieces and demanded another.

Very quickly, Lot built up an impressive collection of torn, tattered and ripped bears. His parents convinced themselves that it was just a silly phase, just a passing fancy, just a passing fanciful silly phase. So they fed Lot's obsession and commissioned every sort of bear that a child could imagine, and Lot demolished them all.

Enormous, puffy bears... *Destroyed.*

Tiny, adorable bears with tiny adorable paws... *Conquered.*

Soft plush bears filled with goose feathers... *Plucked.*

As a toddler, Lot's crib was littered with the stuffing. When he became a boy, his bed was covered by mangled fabric. Finally, when Lot grew into a young man, to the great relief of his parents, he tired of silly, stuffed bears.

Unfortunately, he became obsessed with the real thing.

In his tutoring lessons, Lot had heard tales of distant native populations who marked their step into manhood with the slaying of a full grown bear, and Lot knew immediately that that was the path for him. Suddenly, all of Lot's royal studies were ignored. He no longer cared about the delicacies of international relations or the finer points of court etiquette. He yawned through language lessons. He snoozed through history.

Lot wanted to get his hands on a bear and nothing else mattered.

For their part, Lot's parents had become first-class enablers and had blinded themselves to the fact that their son was exhibiting, to say the least, less than admirable qualities. However, his parents, the upstanding royalty that they were, waved every question and concern aside as they convinced themselves that everything was normal in their lives. It was a technique that had served them well thus far, and they had no intention of changing it up now.

A rainstorm caused flooding in the east wing of the castle?

"It's just a little water. It'll pass."

Famine is spreading quickly amongst your people?

"That's silly. Everything's fine."

Your son is developing into a borderline lunatic with an obsession for bears?

"Not a problem. La-la-la."

So, with barely a second thought, they brought in the finest hunters to train Lot for his first encounter with a bear. Experts in combat were tasked with studying the lumbering beasts, so that Lot could be taught how best to deal with the towering animal he so wanted to face. Lot drank in these lessons with the passion that nothing else could come close to inspiring.

And, just to be safe, the oldest, most hobbled, and half-blind bear they could find was brought in for the big event. Even in this regard, Lot's parents were determined to protect their darling son from all harm.

Finally, on the day of his coronation, the boy got his dearest wish. Surrounded by guards who were ready to jump in at the slightest sign of trouble, Lot lumbered into a small wooden arena with the aged bear and they prepared for battle. At seventeen years of age, Lot had started to resemble his favorite animal. He was a tall, heavy set youth. He had large feet, big thick hands, and he carried most of his weight in his belly. In his training, he hadn't set much store in building his dexterity or speed, instead he focused on strength. And, even for a boy his age, his strength had become prodigious. Lot could lift a full grown man over his head, and then throw that man nearly the length of the dinner table. He didn't hesitate to slap around his riding instructors and generals. The castle servants did their best to avoid him lest they risk being punted around the hallways.

So, despite the fact that all of the gathered spectators held their collective breath in suspense, Lot wasn't the least concerned when he finally fulfilled his wish to tangle with a bear. Lot barely batted an eye as he locked up with the wild animal. He thrilled at the chance to finally prove himself a man as he used all of his strength against the real-life object of his obsession.

A massive 800 pound grizzly bear... *Utterly demolished.*

By this time, even Lot's mother had to grudgingly admit that her son was shaping up to be a menacing brute of a dictator. But it was too late. Lot's father had passed away a few months earlier. There were no other possibilities for male heirs. And no one would've wanted to mess with a seventeen year old who could kill a bear with his bare hands anyway.

King Lot had emerged victorious and his path in life was set.

Many years passed, and King Lot now had to deal with the tedious day-to-day business of running a kingdom. However, after battling a bear, nothing else could elicit the same excitement for him. At first, he tried to balance boring affairs of state with the after hours conquering of other beasts. He imported lions, gorillas, and once even had a chimera shipped in from Greece. He tangled with trolls, goblins, and a rare species of fire-breathing golden retriever. But he always came back to his obsession with bears.

He scoured nearby lands for grizzlies and black bears. He sent for mythical white bears from the freezing poles. He even commissioned sorcerers to create strange breeds of blue, red, and purple bears, simply for the purpose of destroying them, although it was suspected they were actually just common varieties that had their fur dyed.

As the decades passed, he cultivated his identity as the "Bear King," and King Lot's influence and cruelty grew to match that beastly reputation. He began to treat his subjects with harsher and harsher penalties for even minor infractions. He expanded his kingdom by conquering smaller, weaker lands out of a need to prove his own power. And very few neighboring lords were able to stand up to him.

Because, honestly, it's just not that easy to oppose a man who wrestles with bears for fun.

All that changed when Arthur came to power.

King Arthur occupied a kingdom far to the east of King Lot, but Arthur hadn't been content to stay in his own lands. Although he was barely into his adulthood, the young King Arthur had already succeeded in overthrowing Vortigern and his Saxon army. He had weakened the grip of Lord Yder and his Pict mercenaries.

And it was common knowledge that Arthur intended to come for King Lot next.

Slowly but surely, Arthur and his force of young, idealistic knights chipped away at Lot's kingdom and strongholds. Outposts fell. Bordering villages were released from Lot's power. Even his main castle had been overthrown and Lot had been lucky to escape from Arthur's invading forces.

Now King Lot stood atop a tall spiraling fortress, one of the few outposts remaining under his control since the onslaught of Arthur's forces. The fort was small in width, but it rose tall into the sky and its circular construction gave King Lot a clear view of all the surrounding lands. He gazed out into the night and felt the piercing chill breeze. The sparse hair atop his head had long since crept backward so that now he only had a thin crown of white around the edges. It provided little protection against the cool night air. However, he simply pulled his bear skin cloak tighter around his neck and dared whatever the night held in store to try and defeat him.

The wooden baffle that led down from the roof into the fortress below flipped open, and one of Lot's warriors scrambled out. The man was impressively large, well over six feet tall, with the lumbering stature of a bear that King Lot prized in all of his fighters.

"It's not safe for you out here, my lord," the large man warned, "You're far too exposed!"

"Ha! You think, King Lot, is afraid?" said Lot, bristling at the insinuation and feeling the bear head rustle between his broad shoulder blades. "The Bear King fears no one."

"But Arthur may be on his way," said the warrior.

"I welcome Arthur's attack," growled King Lot. "This fortress is impenetrable from land and sea. If he dares to strike me, he will face the full power of-"

However, King Lot couldn't maintain his gravelly demeanor as he asked,

"What is that?"

King Lot pointed off to the east skies where there were over a half dozen large figures zipping through the air. He had never seen beasts that looked so strange. They were like birds, but they seemed to have no need to flap their wings. They also seemed to be flying much too straight and true to follow the normal behavior of a flock of geese.

Also, without a doubt, they seemed to be headed right for them.

"They're too large to be birds..." said the warrior with mounting confusion.

"And what bird flies at night?" added King Lot.

He had a hard time concealing that for the first time in many, many years there was fear in his voice.

~ ~ ~

His golden hair rustling, Arthur cut through the evening sky and rode the breeze upon his strange contraption made of long, wooden poles and a covering of tightly stretched leather. The cold wind danced across his face, but invigorated him as he tore through the black night toward the spiralling fortress that was his goal.

Holding formation to his left on a glider of her own was Guinevere. Her long hair whipped behind her despite being pulled into a long, tight braid that was nearly as thick as her wrist. Arthur glanced over to her and smiled. The look she shot back was considerably less friendly. If Arthur didn't know better, he would've thought Guinevere might've liked to give him a good kick on the chin.

The young king looked over his shoulder and saw six more young men following on leather wings of their own. Each of them was smooth faced but determined. Although none of them were officially knights yet, being too young at the tender age of sixteen, Arthur had chosen them all personally for their promise on the field of battle. He had spent time training with each and every one of them, and had been impressed by their skills with the sword, their abilities for quick thinking and improvisation, and their fearlessness in the face of overwhelming odds. It didn't hurt that they were also all light enough to easily maneuver the gliders.

Nonetheless, all of them looked more than a little uneasy at their current situation soaring hundreds of feet above the ground on little more than tree branches and cowhide.

Arthur had to smile as he turned to Guinevere and shouted,

"When we return, remind me to thank Sir Percival for his brilliant design!"

"Or not!" Guinevere shouted back in a tone that was as cold as the night air.

14

"Why, Lady Guinevere," said Arthur, "Have I finally discovered something that unnerves even you?"

"I admit, I prefer to keep my feet on the ground," said Guinevere, and her voice came out unnaturally shaky, "And, please, don't call me '*lady*.'"

"You're not the queen yet," Arthur reminded her.

"I haven't much use for titles! Even when that day comes... Just Guinevere will do."

Arthur nodded. *Fair enough.*

"Ready to go our separate ways then, Guinevere?" asked Arthur.

Guinevere nodded and then wrenched her glider to the left. It peeled off of the group, and quickly soared away into the distance. Arthur had to admire the deftness with which Guinevere piloted the strange craft despite her distaste for it. He needn't have been surprised, however. It had been almost three years since the two of them had reunited and freed their kingdom from the evil clutches of Vortigern. And Arthur and Guinevere hadn't been idle in that time. They emerged from the rubble of Tintagel Castle more determined than ever. The old castle was unsalvageable after the attack by Vortigern's Red Dragon, not to mention Guinevere's own penchant for explosives. Within months, Arthur set about constructing a new and grander castle. Sir Percival had been appointed chief architect, and the normally nervous knight proudly rose to the occasion.

However, Arthur knew that even more important than building a new castle was building a new kingdom. With Guinevere at his side, they enacted a daring plan to free local lands, offer friendship to like-minded lords, and depose powerful dictators. In the past year alone, Arthur and Guinevere had led raiding parties to weaken the strongholds of nearly a half-dozen villainous warlords. Their exploits had included charges across land and sea.

But this was their first foray into the skies.

As the rhythmic flapping of the leather glider crackled over his head, Arthur couldn't help but grin. This was what he lived for. He torqued his head to look back at the six young knights-in-training following closely on his tail. They were all holding on for dear life. Some maintained more color in their cheeks than others, and some actually seemed to be relishing the flight. Fortunately, each of them had a clear look of determination pasted on their young faces. However, each of them also had at least a glimpse of fear on their faces too. Arthur felt that was only too wise.

"Ready for battle, men?" Arthur called to them.

As one collective unit, they all shouted back, "Huzzah!"

Arthur nodded proudly, then added somewhat to inspire them, and somewhat to fill them with proper caution, "You all wish to be knights one day. Let's see who lives that long!"

The handful of knights-in-training exchanged panicked glances at Arthur's words as they wondered just what they were getting themselves into. Arthur let them wonder as he guided his glider into for a landing atop the rapidly approaching fortress of King Lot.

With his cool athleticism and quick reflexes, King Arthur easily touched down upon the roof and released his glider. The shock at

Arthur's arrival couldn't be more plain upon King Lot's face as the bear king's jaw dropped and he lumbered back in clumsy disbelief. The difference between the two kings couldn't be more apparent. Arthur was young and handsome yet unassuming. If it weren't for his rapidly spreading reputation, no one would have known he was a king by his simple clothing and lack of royal accoutrements. King Lot, on the other hand, was now an old man who chose to cover himself in regal adornments, most notably his garish bear skin cloak.

Moments after Arthur's landing, the half dozen knights-in-training all touched down behind him. Some of their landings were smoother than others, but Arthur was relatively pleased at how well they all availed themselves. Each of them drew their weapons, adjusted their fighting stances, and prepared for battle.

Arthur took the lead, standing in front of his small group, and unsheathed the mighty sword that hung at his hip. Klærent the Stonebourne was the legendary sword that Arthur had drawn from out of solid stone to prove his birthright and to mark his claim on his kingdom. The limestone and marble inlaid into the hilt had become comfortable beneath Arthur's fingers. He had become accustomed to thinking of the sword as an extension of his own arm. Now he had the impressive blade pointed at King Lot.

"How dare you come here to my lair," spat King Lot.

"Come now, Lot. Did you really think you could just hole up in this fortress forever? Especially after all the misery you've caused," said Arthur.

"Do you expect me to simply roll over and join your idealistic vision?" chided King Lot, then adding with a jeer. "Camelot? Ha!"

"I'm offering all the kingdoms a chance to unite," Arthur said. "You would have to pay for your crimes. But there is a place for you. We can all work together."

"Work together! Ha!" boomed King Lot with a mocking tone. "I choose to rule! And I still have my many followers. Guards!"

At the bear king's command several warriors climbed out onto the roof and joined their master. Once again, the differences couldn't be more plain. King Lot had chosen to surround himself with hulking behemoths for allies. Each of his men was towering and bulky with gnarled weapons of spiked clubs and pick axes hefted over their shoulders or clutched in their big hands. Arthur's contingent of knights-in-training were slim and poised with shining swords that they looked well prepared to use. However, Arthur couldn't deny that they also looked much younger. Much, much younger.

"Did you really think you would have the advantage, Arthur?" asked King Lot in a low taunt, "It's not wise to sequester yourself with a bear in his hole."

And then King Lot flipped back his own bear-skinned cloak to reveal large spiked gauntlets. There was one on each hand, and they clearly were meant to give him the appearance of having large, menacing claws. Arthur couldn't deny that the effect was somewhat unnerving, and he could tell by the slight uncomfortable shifts in weight behind him that his young followers felt the same way.

"I am ready to bare my claws," declared King Lot.

He's really going with this bear motif... thought Arthur.

"Your men and your weapons are impressive, but I too have my followers," Arthur said aloud to King Lot as he gestured to the half dozen knights-in-training that stood behind him.

King Lot clearly was not impressed as he said, "The cubs?! They can't be more than fourteen!"

"Sixteen, actually," Arthur corrected him simply. "Yet I agree, that's quite young. Still they've been well-trained. And they assure me they're ready for this."

Arthur turned to his men and surveyed the nervous yet determined looks on each of their faces.

"You are ready for this, right?" Arthur asked.

The knights-in-training all nodded. Although some seemed more confident than others.

"You truly think they stand a chance against the bear king?!" shouted King Lot as he puffed out his impressively large chest.

"We'll find out, won't we?"

And with that, Arthur sheathed Klærent the Stonebourne. Then with an almost impassive manner, Arthur parted the small group of knights-in-training and worked his way to the back of their ranks. A few of them darted their eyes in his direction with apparent confusion.

"Well, go on then," Arthur said to them, and added with simple wave of his hand, "Let's see what you've got. Capture the Bear King."

All six of young knights-in-training were united in a moment of disarray, but they didn't have much time to dwell on it as King Lot and his warriors charged forward and the still night air was filled with the resounding wail of battle. As Arthur watched, the knights-in-training quickly leapt into the fray. Their blades slashed strong and true. Their composure never faltered. They were truly a sight to see.

King Lot and his warriors tried to press their weight and strength down upon the much smaller force, but it was no use. Each of Arthur's knights-in-training were smart enough to not engage. Instead they used their impressive speed and agility. They darted back and forth, easily dodging clumsy yet powerful swings of spiked clubs and pick-axes.

"Nice work, men," said Arthur by way of encouragement. "Be on your guard. Oooh, watch out for those claws!"

As he watched them fight, Arthur couldn't help but swell a bit with pride. The young knights-in-training were all good. A few of them were quite good.

One was excellent.

Over and over again, Arthur found himself drawn to a particularly clean-cut knight with short, neatly trimmed black hair. This young man's technique was flawless as he easily adjusted his fighting style to match whatever warrior he happened to match up with at any given moment. As Arthur looked on, the clean-cut knight began battling two men at once. Arthur watched as the knight-in-training performed a flashy maneuver where he disarmed one man, then neatly caught the attacker's dagger, and stabbed both of his opponents in quick succession.

Arthur smirked as he thought, *Not bad. He'll be one to watch for certain knighthood.*

But Arthur couldn't dwell on the thought too long as he saw another of the knights-in-training fall to one knee. The young man struggled to regain his balance, and in the moment of struggle, one of Lot's warriors charged and was about to bring a particularly nasty looking spiked club down.

Arthur was looking to training these young men, but he didn't want to get them killed. Although he was now a feared and respected king in his own right, it had only been a few years since Arthur himself was sixteen. So he couldn't fault these young men for stumbling a bit. Without a moment's hesitation, Arthur sprung forward and knocked Lot's warrior out with a perfect right cross. The knight-in-training, who only moments ago had been struggling, now looked to his king with thankful admiration.

"What are you smiling about? The fight's not over," said Arthur and he waved his hand to urge the young man back into battle.

The abashed knight-in-training quickly got back to his feet and scrambled into the fight.

Once again, Arthur's attention was drawn back to the clean-cut knight who had now boldly chosen to take on King Lot himself. For a large, older man, the bear king showed surprising speed as he slashed with his gauntlet claws. It looked like it was all the clean-cut knight could do to stay out of King Lot's brutal reach. Slash after slash after slash. King Lot's strength seemed tirelessly, and the clean-cut knight could simply dodge. But then Arthur saw the real game. The clean-cut knight wasn't off balance. He was waiting for the proper opening. Arthur had to be impressed by the young knight-in-training's patience. King Lot attacked again and again, but his young opponent simply waited.

And waited. And waited. And waited…

CRACK!

With a sudden opening in the Bear King's arc, the clean-cut knight-in-training sprung and, with astounding speed and force, threw all his weight into it as he punched King Lot in the sternum. There's was an undeniable crunching noise that rented the night sky, and Arthur watched King Lot's eyes bulge and teeth clench.

The Bear King slumped like a sack of potatoes. Out cold.

Now Arthur was really impressed as he thought, *Forget knighthood. I'll have to be careful not to make this one angry.*

All around, Lot's warriors lay fallen on the ground. And Arthur's gang of young knights-in-training looked pretty pleased with themselves. Broad grins stretched across their handsome faces, and they each puffed out their chests despite clearly being winded by the night's excursions. But they all had a bit of a swagger. And they earned it.

Arthur approached the clean-cut knight who quickly bowed his head. Not without a little surprise, Arthur observed that this young man who had so bravely leapt into battle was actually nervous around his own king.

"How did you do that?" asked Arthur as he pointed to the unconscious lump that was once a mighty king. "I just taught you that move yesterday. And you seem to have already mastered it."

"Well, sir, King Arthur, sir, I watched you closely," said the knight-in-training. Then he added with an embarrassed shrug, "And then I didn't sleep at all last night as I practiced…"

"Well done," said Arthur with a nod, then he turned to the rest of the young men, "Well done to all of you!"

Bursting with excitement and pride, the knights-in-training lifted their swords high in the air and cheered loudly and as one, "Huzzah! Huzzah! Huzz-"

WHOOSH!

The stillness after the battle suddenly vanished as, out of nowhere, a dart struck one of the knights-in-training in the neck. The young man slapped his hand to the dart and drew it out. But it was too late. In an instant, a confused, dazed look crept over his face, his knees gave way, and the knight-in-training crumbled.

The other men sprung to attention, but it was no use. They were already off balance and at-a-loss.

Whoosh. Another dart. Another neck. Another man down.

Their swords were drawn. But this wasn't an enemy they could fight. Or even see.

Whoosh. Dart. Neck. Fall.

In no time flat, the six young knights-in-training were all splayed out on the ground. Some had already succumbed to unconsciousness, some struggled hopelessly to regain their senses. But there was nothing they could do.

Arthur stepped over the clean-cut knight who looked up at his king with eyes that were clearly struggling to focus. Arthur just looked down at him and shook his head.

A moment later, Guinevere stepped out of the shadows and took her place beside Arthur as she tucked a small dart gun into the folds of her cloak.

"I guess they weren't entirely ready, Arthur," she said.

"No. A little too quick to drop their guard, I think. Not quite ready yet," agreed Arthur.

And he watched as the clean-cut knight's head drooped and fell to the ground amongst all his sleeping comrades.

~ ~ ~

The night was heavy and black with the sound of chirping insects and a crackling fire that filled the peaceful evening air. Guinevere lounged and enjoyed her well-earned break. She and Arthur had made plans weeks earlier to test the knights-in-training with her little deception, and Guinevere felt that it was an excellent idea.

Plus, who didn't like playing with a dart gun?

However, what she had failed to foresee was how much work it would end up being afterward. Guinevere and Arthur were left alone to drag the sleeping bodies of six young men who couldn't

24

exactly be considered small out of the conquered fortress. Guinevere liked to consider herself to be in fairly good shape, but this was taxing. Not only that, she and her king also had to bind up King Lot and his men, so that they wouldn't escape before a contingent of Arthur's fully trained knights came to arrest them. Guinevere, who usually felt quite clever, was cursing herself for not at least using the young knights-in-training to clean up after the massive King Lot.

Nonetheless, the work was now done, and Guinevere could relax in the cool night air, beside a roaring fire, with an entertaining show about to begin.

The knights-in-training were all starting to wake up.

And it was hilarious.

Each of them struggled to take stock of their surroundings, but half of them couldn't even lift their heads off of the ground. There was also lots of drooling. At the moment, Guinevere was particularly enjoying watching one knight-in-training with short black hair struggling to sit up, and failing spectacularly. Only minutes ago, Arthur had sung the young man's praises as a force to one day reckon with. However, at the moment, the young man couldn't even lift his head up out of a puddle of mud that he had managed to get himself mired in.

Arthur stepped up beside Guinevere and they both watched as the clean-cut young man used all the strength in his arms to lift himself, and then come splashing back down into the mud.

"Careful," said Guinevere. "That basilik venom may have been diluted, but it'll still take a while to work its way entirely through."

Nonetheless, the clean-cut young man forced himself up onto his feet. And then quickly collapsed back down to the ground. Undeterred, the young man wasted no time before he began to try again.

"This one's a tenacious thing, isn't he?" remarked Guinevere.

"Seems to be," agreed Arthur.

All of the knights-in-training were awake now, and moaning appropriately, so Arthur began to stride amongst them. Guinevere watched eagerly. It was time for one of Arthur's lessons. And she always liked his lessons.

"Ah good, you're all up," said Arthur, "Now, who can tell me how Guinevere and I managed to knock you out and drag you into the woods?"

Each of the knights-in-training attempted a response, but mostly what came out of their mouths could have easily been mistaken for animal noises. There was a lot of groaning, and braying, and somewhat unexpectedly, moooo-ing. There was also still a great deal of drooling.

Arthur pressed on as he said, "All excellent answers, but not the ones I'm looking for. We were able to surprise you all, because you all let your pride get the better of you."

Once again the young men tried to answer, but once again, it mostly just came out as gibberish. Guinevere was fairly certain she heard one young man say, "Horse shoe," although she couldn't imagine why.

"Each and everyone of you got over confident," Arthur continued, "And that can be just as dangerous as being ill-prepared in the first place."

A final time they tried to respond. But it was still no good.

"Don't worry, it happens to the best of knights," said Arthur with a smile, "But, under the worst of circumstances, it can be catastrophic. Since none of you can talk anyway, and since you already had a good long sleep, listen while I tell you a tale."

This was what Guinevere had been waiting for. She settled back against a tree stump, and stretched out her legs. The crackling bonfire was reflected in her gently glowing eyes as she gazed warmly upon Arthur. As much as Guinevere liked Arthur's lessons, she absolutely adored his stories.

"Is it the one about the pirates? Or the cat men of the dale?" she asked eagerly.

"Both good stories. For another time, maybe," said Arthur and he returned her affectionate gaze with one of his own. Then he turned to the knights-in-training still sprawled upon the ground, "But now, my dear fellows, listen closely-"

Guinevere's king, with his golden hair, cleared his throat, and began his tale in a clear, resounding voice,

"Gather all and listen for my tale to begin,

From a time long ago under King Pendragon,

A quest full of magic, of mercy and of might,

Of prideful Sir Gawain and the fearsome Green Knight."

~ ~ ~

CHAPTER 1
Battling with a Giant

The Forests of Broceliade were amongst the darkest, most dangerous, most nightmare infested corners of the world. It wasn't unusual to find secret meetings of sorcerers, or convergences of cutthroat pirates, or rampaging packs of blood-thirsty hellhounds.

And there were always giants.

The most brutal of which was the Black Giant of Broceliade was really more of an ancient ape. It stood thirty feet tall, and was covered by thick black fur all the way down to the tips of its long powerful arms and its almost impossibly large fists. The most unnerving part, however, was its brutish face which bore an undeniable resemblance to a human. On this particular giant, it was an undeniably angry, furious, ferocious human face.

But Gawain didn't seem to be concerned in the least bit.

As he tangled with the towering beast, Gawain struck quite the impressive figure himself. He was tall and strong, although admittedly nothing compared to the giant. His shaggy reddish-brown hair was full and impressive both atop his head and hanging down from his chin as a beard that reached his collar bone. However, the most intriguing aspect of Gawain was his many adornments, trinkets, and talismans. His hair and beard were positively littered with hand-carved Celtic symbols, or colored beads from distant countries, or shining foreign coins collected from far away realms. He even had a shark's tooth woven amongst his thicket of hair. His war-beaten armor was similarly impressive. Nearly every inch was covered with chipped and faded paint depicting Egyptian hieroglyphs or Wiccan spells or ancient, archaic languages whose meanings could only be guessed at. Over the years, Gawain had carefully cultivated this strange collection. Now it filled him with pride, and helped to build his courage.

Because a man had to be courageous to tackle a giant.

"You know, there's something I never quite understood about you giants," said Gawain, by way of a taunt, as he hoped to put the giant off balance.

The giant didn't seem phased as it slammed a massive hand down in an attempt to squish Gawain like a bug as it roared,

"CRUUUUSH!"

Gawain deftly dodged the swipe, and just as quickly, he ducked behind a large tree to give himself a bit of cover.

"You want to pretend you're the biggest, baddest beasts around," said Gawain, continuing his earlier thought, "Flattening people like grapes, and rampaging through villages."

Once again the giant responded with a swing of its battering ram-like hand.

"SMMMMAAAASSHH!"

But the giant's swinging fist only hit the tree that Gawain had hidden behind. Nonetheless, the tree splintered along its mighty trunk, and its base was uprooted. Gawain had to dart away as he continued to taunt the giant.

"But you insist on living in forests surrounded by towering mighty trees."

"FLAAAT!"

Now the giant clasped both of its enormous hands together and pounded its fists into the ground. Gawain leapt backward, but then the courageous knight sprung forward and landed on the giant's outstretched arms. With quick deft movements, Gawain ran up the giant's outstretched limbs and perched upon its shoulders. It was a bold tactic, to be certain, but Gawain had never denied that he was a bold man.

"It's like you want to be reminded how small you really are," said Gawain as he threw his arms around the giant's tree trunk thick neck and squeezed.

"SLLLLAAAAP!"

The giant's wide flat hand slapped at Gawain, and if Gawain was being honest, it hurt. A lot. Yet he hadn't become the greatest knight in the kingdom without enduring his share of pain, so the mighty Sir Gawain ignored it and squeezed ever tighter.

"My theory is that secretly you want to brought down low," continued Gawain with a bit of a groan, "Being big actually scares you."

"AAAACCCKKK!" cried the cruel giant, and Gawain didn't think it was one of the beast's better retorts.

31

The giant swatted again and again at Gawain, but the slaps were becoming weaker and weaker. After a moment, the giant stumbled altogether and fell to one knee.

But Gawain squeezed all the more as he said, "Deep down, you actually know how insignificant you are. And you're just begging to be taken down a notch."

THUD!

With a thundering rumble, the last breath left the once terrible, rampaging giant and it crashed to the ground.

Dead.

Gawain simply jumped off of its back and landed neatly on the ground. Feeling very proud of himself indeed, the successful knight dusted his hands and filled his lungs with rich, victorious air. It was a job well done. He bowed his head to his fallen opponent and said with a shrug,

"You don't have to say anything. I'm pretty sure I'm right."

And with that, Gawain rushed away, because even a knight as great as he was, wasn't foolish enough to stay in a place as dark and dangerous as the Forests of Broceliade any longer than was strictly necessary.

~ ~ ~

It was undeniable that Gawain was a great warrior. He was a master of the sword. His bravery knew no bounds. His exploits on the fields of battle and in wide-ranging quests had nearly reached mythical status.

Lesser known, however, was that he also had a nearly unrivalled ability to celebrate.

Today, he had chosen his favorite tavern, The Griffin's Gather, in his favorite village, Oak's White, that stood in the shadow of his favorite castle, Tintagel, ruled by his favorite king, Uther Pendragon. The tavern was poorly lit with candles that weren't replaced nearly often enough. The tables and bar top were nearly always dirty. The food and drink was mediocre at best.

Yet Gawain loved the place desperately.

And there was a simple explanation for Gawain's deep affection for the tiny tavern, and it was that the people and the place had a deep affection for him. No matter what time of day or year, Gawain could always count on finding someone here that was eager to hear him tell the tales of his many adventures, quests and crusades. More often than not, his audiences consisted of large quantities women, and that made him even fonder of the place. Today was no exception. Gawain sat in the midst of a crowd of mostly women, in the dirty, poorly lit tavern, and the great knight regaled them with the story of his recent victory over the Black Giant of Broceliade.

"And then I dropped that oafish, lop-sided giant! He crashed to the ground and his last thought was, *'I never should've tangled with the great Sir Gawain!'*" declared Gawain with an impressive flourish, then he added with a shrug, "But what he said was just, *'uuuhh.'*"

The crowd laughed and oooh-ed with excitement and admiration, as Gawain lifted his tall, foaming mug of ale and drank

33

it in one impressive go. A tiny dribble of the drink slipped down his lips and snaked through Gawain's impressive beard. The mighty knight, who was the envy of all, wiped it away and let out an impressive belch.

"Oh my, oh my…" giggled a husky yet inviting feminine voice, "I can't believe you were really brave enough to go into the Forests of Broceliade!"

Gawain's eyes fell upon a lovely, young barmaid who gazed upon him with a look bordering between admiration and infatuation. A grin curled around the edges of Gawain's mouth as he gestured for the young woman to sit on his lap. She seemed only too happy to oblige.

"Of course, I was willing to journey into the depths of that accursed forest," said Gawain as he wrapped his strong arms around her soft middle. "A brave knight has got to be willing to journey deep into the darkest, most dangerous of places."

The pretty barmaid settled into his lap, and frowned.

"But, um, I thought you said it was just the outermost edges?"

Gawain stuttered, "Well… Yeah… It was… But I was willing to go deeper, if it was necessary. I'm always willing to do whatever it takes."

His boast did the trick as the barmaid cooed, "You're sooooo brave."

"And you're so beautiful," Gawain replied.

The barmaid giggled at the rugged knight's boldness, and Gawain pulled her in tight. He tipped her back and was about to kiss her when,

"GAWAAAAAIN!"

The startled knight jolted upright and nearly sent the dazed barmaid tumbling off of his lap and onto the floor as he watched an enormous, red-faced man bursting in through the tavern's doors. This in and of itself didn't particularly worry Gawain. The six, equally angry-looking men who followed on the heels of the first man, however, gave Gawain a bit of pause.

"You take your hands off my wife!" shouted the first man.

Gawain cast a glance at the barmaid who was now blushing furiously.

"You're married?!" Gawain cried.

"He's usually a very gentle man..." the barmaid said in a small, tremulous voice.

But at that moment, the furious husband lifted a wooden chair high up over his red face, then with a violent crashing motion, the brute of a man brought the sturdy chair down to the ground and easily reduced the finely crafted sitting apparatus to rubble.

"He's usually very gentle," repeated the barmaid, using particular emphasis to explain her husband's current furious state-of-mind.

For his part, Gawain stayed calm. He was a mighty knight under the great King Uther Pendragon. He'd faced much worse than this. Witches and ghouls and fire ants that really breathed fire and all sorts of weird and wonderful creatures. He wasn't in the least worried about this.

Plus, he had already consumed several strong drinks and felt correspondingly bold.

The noble knight casually ushered the barmaid aside, and then strolled up to face the angry husband and his angry friends.

"Now, everyone just calm down," said Gawain, "I didn't know she was married."

"But you knew my wife was when you met her!" piped in one of the other friends.

"Mine too!" a third chimed in.

However, Gawain maintained control of the situation as he calmly held out his hands to the fuming men.

"I assure you, my good men, they were all honest misunderstandings," said Gawain in his most measured, good-natured tone. "Now, before things get ugly, I'm willing to let all this go. And I will walk out like a gentlemen."

With that, Gawain headed for the door, and all was right with the world. Or it would've been if the angry gang of men had any sense. But one of them just couldn't help himself.

"Coward!"

That did it. No one called Gawain a coward. Who did they think they were? Had they really never heard any of his stories? Did they really know nothing about him? Sir Gawain was many things, but a coward was not one of them. He also wasn't the sort of man to suffer insults from lesser men. And the furious grinding of his teeth showed it.

Gawain spun to face the red-faced horde and growled, "What did you call me?"

The barmaid's husband was only too happy to reply, "I said you're a miserable, shaking, pitiful cow-"

It was destined to be the last thing the man would be able to say for a quite a while as Gawain reared back, dropped his shoulder, and completely laid the man out with a monstrous uppercut. The towering man crumbled backward as he left his feet entirely and crashed onto a table which collapsed under his massive weight.

More of the furniture was soon bound to be demolished as the six angry friends all jumped into the fight and surrounded Gawain.

"I'm the great Sir Gawain! Do you know who I am?!" bellowed the prideful knight as he prepared to show all half-dozen men the legendary power of his fists.

Apparently the six men didn't know what was good for them, though, and they fell upon Gawain all as one. Knuckles met jaws and the tavern was filled with the sound of thunderous cracks. A few of the men fell back, but only momentarily. They kept coming and coming and coming after Gawain.

"I battled the Roman legions!" Gawain roared as he slammed two men together.

But another two men sprang forward and held Gawain's arms in place as a third man jabbed the knight's stomach over and over.

"I vanquished the Viking hordes!" yelled Gawain as he shook off the two men holding him, and lunged forward to grab the third man, lifted him overhead, and tossed him across the room.

Thus another table was destroyed.

But the angry men wouldn't quit. Another leapt forward and blind-sided Gawain with a surprisingly well-executed right cross. Gawain stumbled a bit as stars began to crowd into the edges of his vision.

"I... ejected... the Egyptian..." Gawain tried to boast despite his tongue not completely obeying his command.

Suddenly the group of men converged once again on Gawain. Or more precisely, they converged on his face. Gawain took another hit. And another and another and another. He was slammed into a wall where he was wailed upon by no less than three men. Nonetheless, Gawain didn't panic. He'd been in worse fights than this. He'd come through worse than this. He was the mighty Sir Gawain and he was sure that he'd still emerge victorious.

Of course, Gawain was also wrong sometimes.

"I... I... I..." mumbled Gawain as he struggled to think of the next accolade he could tout, but he couldn't come up with one. Something about the non-stop fists cracking against his skull made it hard to concentrate.

Finally, his knees buckled and Gawain collapsed back against the wall. This was it for him when-

The sounds of trumpets from heaven came blaring down upon them.

In actuality, it was a simple, ordinary trumpet played by a simple, ordinary trumpeter, but Gawain wasn't thinking too clearly at the moment. Nonetheless, the unexpected blast of the brass horn caused the angry gang of men to stop their onslaught and search around for the source. They quickly locked eyes on a trumpeter dressed in an official tunic that bore the crest of King Uther Pendragon. And that wasn't all.

A moment later, King Uther Pendragon himself strode into the tavern. And the humble watering hole was filled with gasps of astonishment. Most of these men were common people. They worked hard all day long in the fields or at their various trades as blacksmiths or dairymen. It wasn't often that they saw royalty. And King Uther Pendragon with his golden-flecked armor and regal red cape was quite an impressive example of royalty. The half-dozen men could be forgiven for gaping in amazement at this unexpected treat.

One of them even blurted out, "Holy god!"

"No, just a king," said Uther Pendragon and even the deep tenor of his voice radiated royalty. "Although I do try to be pious."

After a few more moments of dismay, one of the men finally connected his brain to his knees and bowed down before the monarch. Quickly each of the other men realized their mistakes and they too bowed down on one knee to their king.

Gawain, however, just slumped down the wall and collapsed to the ground.

"You may all go," said Uther.

39

The men couldn't leave fast enough. A mad dash ensued as everyone bolted for the door. Within an instant, the entire tavern was cleared out. The tall, handsome king strode across the room and looked down on his loyal knight and friend, Sir Gawain, who didn't look so good at all. In fact, he looked rather like a scoop of mashed raspberry jelly that hadn't been spread across its toast yet.

Nonetheless, Gawain did his best to retain his dignity as he proudly proclaimed, "I'm the... great... Sir Gawain..."

And he promptly blacked out.

~ ~ ~

CHAPTER 2

The Story of King Uther Pendragon

As the last rays of sunshine hid themselves away at the edges of the earth, King Uther Pendragon stood atop the tallest tower of Tintagel Castle and surveyed his vast kingdom. From this height he could gaze out and see or imagine seeing over impossible distances. He saw plains, lakes, valleys, and forests. And he knew that, as remarkable as it might seem, he was responsible for it all.

Uther shivered slightly as his breath came out in an icy cloud on the cold winter's air. Yet he drew another deep breath and imagined that he was taking in just a small bit of his entire country that was somehow his.

From a young age, Uther had preferred to live a simple, unambitious life. He knew that one day he would rise to royalty, but he never had great plans for the grand eventuality. He had no desire to emulate Caesar or Alexander the Great. Uther just wanted to keep things running more or less smoothly. Generally, as a boy he had done just enough in his studies to learn the basics. He presented himself just well enough to look capable. He sought out the average, and never strove to be great.

He should've realized that, with a name like Uther Pendragon, greatness was assumed.

Without even meaning to, Uther's name became one that was synonymous with an awesome mystique. It all started simply enough, with Uther's love of playing tricks, pranks and half-truths. At nine years of age, Uther Pendragon started a rumor that his surname was a secret nod to the fact that his family did, in fact, have a dragon hidden away deep in a cave system beneath the land. A sleek, majestic white dragon. Uther spun impressive yarns about how they had to secretly feed it with wagons full of corn that the dragon roasted with its flames causing the small, yellow kernels to burst into bits of white fluff that the great scaly beast then devoured in massive quantities. The young man said the white dragon only flew at night and went so high into the sky that it seemed to be a distant blur. Then Uther would point to shooting stars and claim that it was actually the dragon soaring high above them. One by one, he convinced all the other young children, until it was a commonly held "fact" that the Pendragons were the proud owners of a real dragon. Alone in his chambers, Uther giggled maniacally at the complicated legend he had managed to create.

As he grew older, Uther continued to weave more and more sublime stories. He proudly boasted of how his ancestors still rode through the countryside on the backs of mammoths in the spring planting wild-flowers wherever they went. He invented journeys that he had taken to Atlantis down in the depths of the sea. He regaled the other boys about epic romances that Uther had conducted with magical enchantresses from far, foreign lands, and the illegitimate children he may or may not have roaming about.

Some of his stories were mostly true, some were stretches of fancy. and some bore no resemblance whatsoever to reality. And slowly but surely an amazing version of Uther Pendragon began to emerge from the stories. Although the real Uther had very little actual ambition, the fantasy Uther was quickly becoming a figure of astounding deeds and influence.

When he had turned eighteen, Uther set out to create his greatest prank yet.

He had come up with a scheme to create a strange, exotic arrangement of stone monoliths in the middle of a barren countryside. Then he'd be able to tell any number of stories about strange creatures from the starry night skies that had placed them there, or ancient societies who had used the bizarre circle for pagan worships. Uther's mind absolutely spun at all of the possibilities. However, his first problem was how to build it. He couldn't exactly drag big stones around the countryside on his own. And he couldn't use servants, because he had learned from an early age that the best way to ruin a story was by bringing too many people into it.

Uther needed a wizard.

After careful searching and quiet cajoling, the young man who would be king stumbled across an old, strange man with a long, gray beard and a tall, knotted wooden staff. Merlin, for that was the old man's name, chose to mostly speak in rhymes which was frustrating but it seemed to help him perform amazing magic, so Uther didn't complain too much. After a few simple displays of magic, Uther was completely satisfied and he quickly took the wizard into his service. In the dead of night, the young man and the old wizard stole out of the castle and raced into the uninhabited countryside.

Uther watched with mounting glee as Merlin stood in the midst of the open field, raised his wooden staff and spoke in his strange, musical voice,

"Come mighty rocks

From place unknown

And dance as one

In Hendge of Stone!"

Then, even more strangely, the old man began to twist and contort himself in the middle of the field. At first, Uther thought that Merlin might be having some sort of a fit, but as the wizard kicked up his feet and waved his arms, Uther realized he was witnessing a strange and magically jig. Even more unbelievable was when massive rectangular stones began to soar into the field as if they were lighter than the wind itself. The rocks were tall and almost uniform in their shape and they playfully arranged themselves into the most unusual structures. Some lay perpendicular across others. Others stood alone as sentries against the night. Altogether the formed almost a perfect circle.

It was amazing.

When it was all finished, Uther hooted and cheered at the spectacular sight. This was truly going to be the stage for his greatest stories yet.

But the old wizard strode up to the young Uther and placed a hand on his shoulder as he spoke.

"Splendid. Spectacular. Singularly wondrous. This is quite an achievement you have devised, young Uther Pendragon," said Merlin. "I wonder what other grand and remarkable things you might be able to achieve if you were only to put your great mind to it."

Uther just laughed. He couldn't have been less interested.

But the wizard pressed on, "You may scoff now. But boys must also always become men one day. And sometimes much sooner than they might expect…"

Sure enough, Uther returned home at sunrise the next morning and two surprises awaited him. The first was the sad and terrifying news that his father had passed away in the night and Uther was now king. The second was the happy and equally terrifying news that he had a child on the way.

The next nine months passed in whirlwind of official coronations and head-spinning strategy sessions. Uther met with foreign dignitaries and local officials, and he didn't remember even half of their names or faces. The formerly boring business of rule that Uther had previously waved off with a yawn was quickly becoming a nightmare-inducing reality. Scarier still was his queen's quickly growing belly, and faster than Uther could've believed possible, she was giving birth to their beautiful baby son, Arthur.

As he held the baby boy in his arms, Uther realized that he mustn't only make a better kingdom for the infant. He must make a better world.

Suddenly and very quickly, Uther Pendragon's great potential began to be realized. He struck deals with nearby kingdoms to improve living conditions of their mutual countries. With the wizard's help, Uther devised grand strategies for dealing with many of the strange, magical beasts that plagued the lands. And he created a mighty, shining army of knights to help him execute his visions for a greater and more peaceful world.

Now, as Uther stood atop the tower of his grand castle, one of his most loyal and trustworthy knights was stirring at his feet, and quickly coming around to consciousness. Groggily, Sir Gawain awoke and by the sharp groan that escaped his lips, Uther was certain that the recent bar fight had left its mark on the mighty knight.

"I must say, you've looked better, my friend," said Uther.

"Seven to one odds aren't good," groaned Gawain as pushed himself into a seated position, "Especially when you don't have any armor. Or weapons. And you're more than a little drunk."

"Hopefully, you'll be better behaved when my foreign dignitaries arrive," said Uther.

"Put me in any tournament against any fighter and you know I'll do you proud," Gawain responded as he found the small bowl of water and the towel that had been set aside for him. He began to dab at his many cuts and bruises as he cleaned the dried blood off of his face.

"Mmmm... I'm not so sure," said Uther. "There's some young knights even in this kingdom that you seem to be avoiding."

Gawain nearly dropped the wet towel as he cried, "You mean, what's his name...?! Lancelain? Bragsalot? Mark my words, I'll take him down a peg."

Then the brave knight added under his breath, "We just haven't crossed paths yet..."

Uther Pendragon fell silent for a moment. These were the moments he hated as a king. It wasn't an easy job. A king didn't get to have casual friendships. A king wasn't able to simply wave away his friends' faults. A king had to expect more, he had to hold people to a higher standard, and he had to punish those who came up short.

"Sir Gawain, you've been a loyal knight, and a true friend," Uther began, "But if you continue on your path, I'll have to dismiss you."

"Over a bar fight?!" cried Gawain.

"It's far more than a bar fight," said Uther, being careful to keep his tone strong and commanding. "You also slew the Black Giant of Broceliade against my express wishes."

"The giant was on a rampage," said Gawain.

"And something needed to be done, I don't disagree," Uther said with a nod. "But it was also helping to close the northern borders against the Saxons. You know Vortigern is looking for a chance to invade."

Strangely enough, as Uther had sought for greater cooperation and peace among the kingdoms, he also seemed to make more and more enemies. Of all of King Uther Pendragon's many foes, Vortigern and his Saxon army was quickly becoming the most troublesome. They frequently raided Uther's weaker outposts. They made a point of rallying other opposing forces to their banner. Uther had tried to extend a hand of friendship, even going so far as to send Merlin as an envoy, but it had all been to no avail. Vortigern seemed to be that most pesky of antagonists who had no desire to compromise or seek solutions. He only wanted power.

"He- But- The giant was a menace!" argued Gawain bringing the conversation back to the relatively unimportant beast.

Uther sighed as he tried to lay things out for his friend, "You fail to see the larger picture. You rush into battle. Seeking glory. But I seek to unite the kingdoms. I seek to bring all of the kings together so that we might build a new and stronger society. It will not be an easy task. Kings don't always settle for common ground. Which is why it is so important that my own knights be beyond reproach."

Gawain's mighty head drooped and his thick, shaggy reddish-brown hair formed curtains around his face as if to hide his shame. It was clear that he was beginning to understand Uther's point. The king would've liked to leave it there, but he felt that he must continue on.

"Not only that, but Arthur has just turned sixteen," said Uther.

"Sixteen?! My god, he's nearly a man," Gawain said in surprise.

"Yes. And he needs guidance," continued Uther. "He needs good and virtuous knights that he can look up to. Not men simply driven by their pride."

"It wasn't pride! It was a bit of fun at the tavern, and the giant was a bit of admittedly ill-planned heroism," said Gawain.

"Arthur will need much better than that. I'm sorry to say, but he'll need much better than the beaten, beleaguered knight that sits before me now," and Uther's face darkened as he added, "Because one day, he'll face a grave and terrible destiny. One day, he'll have to be king."

Gawain sought the eyes of his king, but Uther once again gazed out toward the darkening horizon and refused to meet Gawain's glance.

Nonetheless, Gawain stated confidently, "Arthur won't be king for a long time yet."

The true and loyal knight tilted his head slightly to try and catch Uther's eyes once more. However, King Uther Pendragon had thought more about this than Gawain could've ever understood. In his many campaigns, Uther had seen other royal men brought down by their arrogance and pride. He had watched as kings who thought themselves invincible ended up alone and friendless in the mud. When Uther had assumed the throne himself, he was well aware that it was a temporary job.

"In our profession, we don't always live to be old men," Uther said. "And we don't always get to come to a glorious end."

Once again, Gawain's head drooped sadly, and once again, Uther was sure that he had made his point.

But enough was enough. There would be time for darkness and there would be time for gloom, but that time needn't have been just then. The good king pushed a bright smile onto his regal face, and some of his deeply etched wrinkles softened. He forced a laugh and waved it all away.

"Come now, old friend. Let's forget about the inevitability of our destiny for a night. Let's put it all behind us," said Uther as he clapped an arm across his friend's shoulder, "The winter feast is about to begin."

~ ~ ~

CHAPTER 3

The Uninvited Guest

The grand feasting hall was packed with happy revellers eager to celebrate the end of another year and greet the coming of a new one. And appropriately a raucous affair was well underway.

Moonlight sparkled in through towering stain-glassed windows bathing the long room in shades of blue, green and red. The rest of the light was provided by dozens of crackling torches whose flames jumped and danced merrily from their brackets on the wall. Tall statues lined the walls and were buffed to a fine shine. And a long table strained under massive loads of food and drink. There were roasted pigs and turkeys alongside overflowing baskets of rolls. Steaming, flaky fruit pies sat beside tall, elaborately decorated cakes. And there were bubbling, frothy, fizzy drinks all around.

Well over a hundred boisterous men were packed into the feasting hall, and they each clutched large foaming beer mugs and gnawed upon enormous turkey legs. Grease and happiness dripped plentifully down each of their joyous faces. Several attractive ladies rushed to and fro as they served more food and spirits to the insatiable men. More than once, the women had to slap away playful hands from happy men reaching for something that wasn't on the menu.

51

And the raucous feasting song of the men reverberated through the mighty stone hall as they sang:

"Throw open the doors and bring out the feast,

We've rescued the ladies and battled the beasts,

We've slain all the dragons,

So fill up our flagons,

Bring out the beer, the rolls, the meat,

We're hungry men and we must eat!"

Near the far end of the table, Gawain was showing off his prowess when it came to celebrating. He had packed his plate high with delicacies, but was now ripping a generous chunk from a turkey leg. As he chewed on the tender meat, he lifted his beer mug and sloshed at least as much down his front as he managed to get in his mouth. Nonetheless, he happily sang along with the other men:

"Bring beer made of barley, and bread made of wheat,

Bring honey-glazed boar so tender and sweet,

We've shed all our mail,

Now bring us more ale,

Then send the puddings, pies, and treats,

We're famished knights and we must eat!"

A particularly lovely lady rushed past Gawain with a new basket of steaming rolls. As she passed, she smiled and winked at Gawain. He wasn't nearly as subtle as he cast her a broad smile in return. She blushed and hurried away, but it was clear that Gawain may have just made plans for later in the evening. He laughed to himself as he sang:

"Line our long table with meat, bread and cheese,

52

Mutton, and turkey, and ham, as you please,

We've faced all our fears,

Now top off our beers,

We'll pound our forks and stomp our feet,

We're starving warriors,

We're famished knights,

We're hungry men and WE MUST EAT!"

Everyone cheered and laughed as the song died away, but the mirth continued on just as strong as ever. The air was thick with the fumes of good food and good friendship. It seemed destined to be a night that all would remember. And it was. It just wouldn't be remembered in the way they had expected.

BOOM!

With an astounding crash, the ten-foot tall ornate doors that led into the feasting hall swung open. Each of the doors weighed nearly a ton, and could usually only be opened by a team of servants working in accord, but now they were thrown open with shocking ease. And how this remarkable feat was achieved was soon made clear as a towering, bull of a man strode into the hall.

The knight, who now had every eye upon him, was unlike any knight that had stepped foot in this feasting hall before. He stood at least seven feet tall, probably taller. He was broad as an ox with enormously thick arms and legs barely covered by impressive armor that seemed both familiar and strangely foreign. Upon his back was a double-headed ax that looked as if it could cleave down even the sturdiest tree in a single blow.

But the strangest part about the man was that, from head to toe, he glowed an otherworldly shade of emerald green.

Silence fell over the great hall as everyone warily surveyed this new entrant. For his part, however, the towering knight strolled casually through the room, as if he had not a care in the world, and headed directly for King Uther Pendragon who sat at the head of the long table. Beneath the table, Gawain's hand fell to his sheathed sword. Something wasn't right here, and Gawain was, as always, at the ready for whatever might happen. But, Uther's recent strictures stuck in his head, and he vowed to wait for his king's command.

"I did not mean to halt your revelries!" boomed the glowing knight, and his voice managed to come off as both pleasant and threatening all at once, "Please let me join you!"

With a forceful swipe, the massive knight snatched a tall mug of beer out of the hands of a gaping man. Then in one impressive go, the strange green knight tossed back his head and drained the entire mug. Without so much as a "thank you" he tossed the empty cup unceremoniously down. Then he locked eyes on the head of the table, and he slowly made his way toward Uther who sat upright and still as he watched this unnatural new guest.

"The great King Uther Pendragon!" cried the knight and he spread his arms wide as if to embrace the king. "What an honor!"

"And might I have the pleasure of your name, sir?" asked Uther pleasantly, although it couldn't be missed that he had refused to stand for the uninvited knight. "So that I might properly greet you."

"I am known simply as The Green Knight. A man whose might and strength is world renowned," proclaimed the knight who was, true to his name, covered in that unearthly shade of emerald.

"I fear I haven't heard of you," said Uther.

"I'm known mostly in the braver quarters of the world," rejoined the Green Knight.

The subtle insult didn't go unnoticed, and many of the men began to grumble. Gawain gripped his sword tighter and he suspected he wasn't the only one to do so. However, Uther Pendragon raised a hand to silence them, and the rabble died away.

"We're always willing to welcome a brave knight," said Uther as he extended a hand and gestured to an open seat about halfway down the banquet hall, "Sit and share our table."

"I would much rather share in your festivities," the Green Knight said with a grin. "King Uther Pendragon, I challenge you to a duel."

Once again, the many men were at attention, and once again, Uther raised a hand to halt them. Although it was clear that this time it took much more restraint on everyone's parts, all of the knights in attendance stayed dutifully in their seats.

"That's not what our celebration entails today," Uther said, "I'm afraid I must decline your-"

"Because you're a coward," cut in the Green Knight.

The rabble was louder than ever. Gawain and several other men rose to their feet, and Gawain even had his sword drawn a half of a foot out of its sheath before their king's voice boomed through the hall.

"SIT DOWN!" shouted Uther and all of his knights obeyed the command. "No one shall rise to his challenge. No one shall give him that power."

King Pendragon's forceful tone was abundantly clear. And everyone obediently sat. Everyone except for the Green Knight who seemed to be relishing the effect that he had upon all the strong men gathered in the feasting hall.

"This is my castle and my hall," said King Uther Pendragon in a clear, ringing tone. "I offered you the hand of friendship. But now I ask you to leave."

"Because you're afraid of me?!" chided the Green Knight.

All eyes were on Uther again. Gawain gritted his teeth as he silently begged Uther to give him the word. How Gawain longed to show this monstrous green brute the slicing edge of his sword. But Gawain was doomed to disappointment as Uther maintained his calm and measured tone.

"Because it is my right as the king to refuse you."

The Green Knight wasn't yet satisfied, however, as he jeered, "The fearful king. The frightened, weakling king. The quaking, quivering, cowering-"

"ENOUGH!"

And this time it was Gawain's voice that rattled through the echoing, high-vaulted hall. The proud knight got to his feet and was quickly cutting the distance between himself and the menacing

Green Knight. Gawain was furious. He was in rage that he had rarely felt before, and he barely registered the shouts of his king.

"Gawain, sit!"

But Gawain failed to heed his king's orders as he strode over to face the towering Green Knight. Gawain wasn't a small man and yet he only reached the shoulders of the massive Green Knight. It couldn't have concerned him less.

"No man talks about my king like that, and lives to tell the tale," growled Gawain.

"Ah, the mighty Sir Gawain, is it?" said the Green Knight as if he expected them to be friends. The Green Knight even had the gall to extend a hand out to Gawain, but Gawain slapped it away.

"Gawain, don't-!" demanded Uther, but he was too late.

"I accept your duel," said Gawain and the words were out of his mouth before Uther had a chance to stop him.

Gawain locked eyes with his king and both of their gazes blazed with fury, but for very different reasons.

"I'll defend your honor, my liege," said Gawain.

For his part, Uther pounded his fist down on the table in frustration. A duel had been accepted. An agreement was in place. Now it had to be seen through.

The Green Knight grinned and laughed as he spoke, "So, brave Sir Gawain, you consent to act as the guardian of this kingdom's fate?"

"I'll be the guardian of this kingdom's honor against the likes of you," replied Gawain with a sneer.

Suddenly an unnatural flash of green light illuminated the stain-glassed windows of the hall. An electricity hung in the air as if lightning had just struck the spot where they had all very recently been enjoying a meal. The tiny hairs on Gawain's arms stood on end, and he felt down into his bones that he had just struck a devil's deal. And he liked it. Bring on the challenge.

Gawain grabbed his sword and was in the process of drawing it when the Green Knight raised a hand in pause. The towering beast of a man laughed as he addressed Gawain.

"Ho! We haven't come to terms yet! We're still civilized men, Sir Gawain. We must have rules," stated the Green Knight plainly.

"Name them, and let's get on with it," said Gawain.

"I have but one small condition," said the Green Knight and then he added with a patronizing nod, "I'm sure a noble man such as yourself will agree."

"I'll meet any challenge you set before me," said Gawain refusing to return the bow.

"Today we duel on your grounds. In one year and one day, you must meet me for a rematch in my realm," was the Green Knight's request.

"Done," said Gawain without a moment's consideration. "Although once I'm finished with you, I don't expect you'll be in any fit condition for a rematch in a year or at any other time."

"Excellent. So we duel."

Gawain's face became serious and his jaw tightened as he drew his long, broadsword from out of its sheath and gripped it tightly with both hands. He watched as the Green Knight almost casually took his massive double-headed ax from off his back. For a moment, the two knights circled slowly and sized each other up. The Green Knight maintained the same jovial smile that he had worn nearly since his entrance. Gawain's face, however, tightened as his lips became thin and his brow furrowed as he fixed into his mind his unfailing rule for battle. Gawain had always had this simple strategy for winning and it had always proved to be true,

Just keep getting up. He could never lose as long as he kept getting up.

The Green Knight reared back to swing his mighty ax, and as Gawain planted his feet to return the blow with his broadsword, he repeated his battle mantra in his head.

Just keep getting up.

Gawain had fought a bull once that charged unexpectedly and gored him.

Just keep getting up.

One time he stumbled into a pit of razor-toothed lemmings.

Just keep getting up.

Now, Gawain's sword met the Green Knight's ax in an epic clash of steel that rattled every cup upon the long dinner table, and the force of the blow sent Gawain careening backward until he crashed against the far wall and crumbled into a pained heap.

But he got up.

And he kept fighting. It was true that, from time to time, Gawain had lost a fight. However, he refused to think about those times, because he had learned the lesson that those battles had provided. Each of those rare occasions had one thing in common. Gawain had failed to keep getting up. He wouldn't make that mistake again.

Gawain took a swipe at the Green Knight and his tall opponent had to leap back to avoid the blow. But the Green Knight swung his ax once more and the vicious arc of the weapon nearly cut off the head of several of the onlookers. Gawain realized that there was too much potential for the onlookers to be hurt, and he made perhaps not the wisest choice. He decided to move the fight outside. He charged at the Green Knight and wrapped his arms around the mighty tree trunk middle of the emerald man. They both tumbled backward and crashed through the tall stain-glassed window that depicted Sir Samuelson the Simple feeding a pack of hungry lambs.

There was a shower of sparkling shards of multi-colored glass and Gawain and the Green Knight fell out into the cold winter's air. Falling, falling, falling. They fell some twenty feet before they crashed in a pile onto the hard sloping roof below. The fall had been a long one, but there was still a long way further to go. The roof stood fifty feet from the ground below. Any wrong step could be their last.

But Gawain got up. And he kept fighting.

A delicate dance ensued between Gawain and the Green Knight. Each of them balanced precariously as they took swipe after dangerous swipe at one another. Gawain dodged a blow from the mighty ax. The Green Knight ducked away from the long broadsword.

"I must say, this is a most thrilling duel, my dear Sir Gawain," said the Green Knight as if he were discussing a game of badminton. "I wonder how much longer you can keep it up?"

"I'll keep going as long as you keep coming," said Gawain, and he was suddenly feeling very bold.

Gawain had been in enough duels and fights to the death to recognize weakness when he saw it. When an opponent stopped to talk, whether it be to cast insults or to make compliments, it was a sure sign that they were tiring. The Green Knight had just shown his hand to Gawain. Gawain knew that it wouldn't be much longer now, and he simply would have to keep up the fight a bit longer before the chance to end it would present itself.

Of course, that was before he stepped onto the patch of ice.

As his feet went out from under him, Gawain lurched forward and took one more desperate swipe at the Green Knight. It was all too easy for the tall emerald warrior to step out of the way, however. Nonetheless as Gawain slipped off of the roof, he had just a moment to glimpse a remarkable sight. The Green Knight willingly leapt off after Gawain and they both careened out into the cold air.

Unlike the Green Knight's controlled jump, though, Gawain was freely tumbling through the air. Falling, falling, falling, once again. But this time he had nothing as welcoming as a roof to look forward to. Fifty feet below him was the castle's moat. During the spring or summer, he could position the fall just right and enjoy the relatively soft water's embrace. But now, in the dead of winter, the moat was frozen over and decidedly unfriendly. Nonetheless, Gawain spun himself and thrust his feet forward to take the brunt of the blow. With only a moment to appreciate it, Gawain watched as the Green Knight somehow landed softly upon the icy surface and looked ready to battle on.

Gawain wouldn't have it so easy.

Fortunately, the frozen surface of the moat broke as Gawain slammed down upon it and he went under. Unfortunately, now he was gripped by the bitter cold of the icy water. Every bit of him screamed as the freezing liquid surrounded him and flooded into every warm space. In an instant, his arms and legs were heavy and leaden. His hands clenched and froze into hard claws. His clothes became sodden and dragged him down further and faster, to say nothing of the heavy broadsword that was now frozen in his hand. He couldn't move from the bitter cold as he sank slowly down to the bottom of the dark moat and landed with a soft thud upon the muddy bottom. He couldn't breathe. He couldn't fight. He couldn't move.

But he could still think. And one thought resounded over and over in his head.

JUST... GET... UP!

Gawain's feet touched the bottom of the icy canal, and with all the strength he had left in him, he squatted and pushed off. He thrust his sword forward and it cleared the way as he smashed upward through the icy surface of the moat. His freezing, sodden body leapt upward and his feet found a remarkably solid bit off ice and standing before him was the Green Knight with a look that was strange mix of terror and delight.

As the Green Knight's paused for a moment to marvel at Gawain's miraculous emergence from the ice, Gawain saw his opportunity. He squeezed his sword in his frozen fingers, and although he could barely feel the handle through his numbness, he swung with all his might.

The perfect powerful slash found its mark.

The Green Knight's mighty head was cleaved from his tremendous towering body.

Gawain finally allowed himself to shiver violently from the terrible cold. He dropped his sword and was about to rush back indoors to find the delicious warmth of a fire. However, as he turned to do so, he saw Uther followed by crowds of people as they emerged from the castle and stood on the lowered drawbridge. Gawain made to join them, but then he registered their gaping, horrified faces.

Something was very, very wrong.

It was now Gawain's turn to wear a look of amazed disbelief and gut-wrenching terror as he pivoted and watched the Green Knight's body casually bending over to pick up its own displaced head.

"An excellent duel, Sir Gawain," said the Green Knight as he positioned his head under his arm in a garish spectacle. "Most thrilling. I will very much look forward to our rematch."

"Wuh-what?! No! You deceived me!" cried Gawain. "I'm not fighting you again!"

"You've declared yourself guardian of this kingdom," the Green Knight reminded him and his tone was still surprisingly cordial considering it came from a decapitated head. "Its fate, and the fate of all its people, lands, and beasts are now bound to you. If you fail to appear in a year's time, then this kingdom falls to me."

Gawain's jaw dropped. He turned and caught Uther's eye, it couldn't have been clearer that the king was furious.

Suddenly, the Green Knight began to fade away into a thin green mist.

"Until that time, Sir Gawain, I bid you farewell," boomed the Green Knight.

"Wait! Where can I find you in a year and a day?" called Gawain desperately.

"Ah, but that wasn't part of our deal. You must do better when setting the terms of your bargains. Yet I'm sure a clever man such as yourself can deduce the location in the next twelve months. Til then, my friend…"

And the the Green Knight was gone, as he almost anti-climactically vanished in a quickly dispelled wisp of green, but left a terrible weight to rest upon the head of the prideful Sir Gawain.

~ ~ ~

CHAPTER 4
Time Slows For No Man

After several hours of warming his stiff, cold limbs in front of a large roaring fire, alone with nothing but his own dreadful thoughts, Gawain finally returned to his chambers. They were small and simple and Gawain had always liked them. He wasn't the most educated man, but he had studied the ancient techniques of the Greek armies, and now he modelled his living quarters on that of the Spartans. They had lived in tiny rooms that were only big enough to house the absolute essentials, and Gawain's was that like too. There was merely a narrow bed, a single chair and one window that faced the eastern rising sun. This was all a warrior needed. However, Gawain broke with the Spartan example after that. His tiny room was filled with scattered prizes, trophies and memorabilia from his many triumphs and journeys. The window ledge was dotted with tiny hand-carved statuettes, given to him by grateful children whom he had saved. Golden chains and ribbons from his thrilling wins in the tournament arenas hung off the posts of his bed. Vials of enchanted water, strange weapons preferred by distant tribes, spare coins pressed in brass or gold bearing the faces of foreign gods, and dried flowers given to him by besotted ladies were all strewn into various corners of the room.

At first, Gawain cast a rueful eye upon them all as he returned to his chambers in the deep hours of night after his duel with the Green Knight. They seemed to be a reminder to him that he was once a great knight and his greatness had dimmed. Or worse yet, perhaps he was never a good knight and these were all misplaced gifts of affection for a man who had never deserved it.

But the longer he gazed upon them the more Gawain's heart warmed.

He remembered the many deeds that he had accomplished for men, women and children that had truly needed him. He reminisced about the beasts he had slain to free villages. Finally, he smiled, and lay down in his bed. He was already feeling better as he recited in his mind that he had been through worse than this and come out the better for it. He was a good man. He was a great knight. This would simply be another one of his glorious adventures. He had nothing to worry about. And, anyway, it was still a full year until he had to see the Green Knight again.

With that happy thought, Gawain relaxed and fell into a deep peaceful slumber that would help to refresh and warm him through the rest of the cold winter nights.

Slowly the days began to get longer and warmer. The moat thawed and the ice thinned and eventually disappeared. The trees outside of the castle began to sprout tiny green buds, and the grass upon the fields started to come back as sunshine broke through the gray winter and warm breezes replaced the frozen winds.

Gawain gray mood was vanished to be replaced by a refreshed and joyful attitude as the winter gave way to spring. Warm weather meant new life. It meant new challenges.

It meant tournaments.

This gave Gawain the great joy of being able to get out his old armor again. And what a sight that armor was. Dented and scratched and beaten by many battles and adventures, yet Gawain absolutely refused to pound the imperfections away. He was able to look at them as points of well-earned pride. Beyond that, his armor was covered with faded chipped paint that Gawain had accumulated in his journeys to distant lands. It bore colorful interlocking symbols and runes and protection spells that made Gawain feel as though he could take on any challenge and win.

It was also really popular with the crowds.

As the spring reached its glory, Gawain found himself once again in the tournament arena to show off his prowess with the sword. He was dressed in that unmistakable armor and he was surrounded by wooden stands that were packed with cheering fans. At the far end of the slightly oval arena, a small yet regal platform was constructed with opulent curtains and a wooden ornate throne in which sat King Uther Pendragon. As the king, he couldn't show favoritism toward any of the knights. But Gawain was quite certain that, if he could, Uther would be cheering for him.

At the moment, a thrilling test of battle was underway. Gawain and three other men were locked into combat. Or, more precisely, Gawain was locked into combat with three other men who had chosen to team up against him in the hopes of toppling the mighty knight.

Gawain wasn't having any of it.

"Come now, lads! Three against one doesn't seem exactly sporting!" chided Gawain.

But the three men pressed down on him anyway, and Gawain wasn't one to shrink before a challenge. As one of the men charged, Gawain spun and grabbed the man's arm thus slinging the man into one of the other two challengers. They collided with a resounding rattle of armor, and collapsed.

The crowd cheered and roared at the display.

And Gawain was only too happy to turn to his adoring fans and urge them on. He raised his arms, and the applause became deafening. Probably too loud, since it obscured the sound of the third challenger's rattling armor as the man took the opportunity to rush at Gawain and tackle him to the ground.

"Can't a guy have a moment to work the crowd?!" groaned Gawain as he twisted from the man's grasp.

Then, with the hilt of his sword, Gawain cracked the third challenger's helmet. From the deep impression left in the heavy steel hat, Gawain was fairly certain he wouldn't have to deal with that man again. Sure enough, the man rolled off and lay in an unconscious heap on the ground.

Despite his bulky armor, Gawain leapt to his feet just in time to see the other two men finally disentangling themselves from one another. They both raised their swords and prepared to attack. This time, Gawain was ready to put on a real show. He gripped his long, heavy broadsword in both hands and ran to meet his challengers. With the ringing sound of tempered blade on tempered blade, Gawain expertly defended against their feeble attacks. His sword blazed in the sunlight and in almost no time at all, he had disarmed both of the men. Then with a crushing finality, Gawain slammed the two men's heads together, and they collapsed and the fight was over.

The crowd couldn't get enough of it as they chanted Gawain's name at the top of their lungs.

Gawain took off his helmet and raised it high in salute to the people. Then, wiping his brow, Gawain turned to the king's platform to see Uther smirking at Gawain as Uther clapped along with everyone else.

Just as Gawain suspected, it was pretty clear that Uther had been rooting for Gawain all along.

Mere moments later, Gawain had stripped off his heavy, hot plates of outer armor and now stood before the small but ornately decorated platform that was reserved for the king and his court. Uther descended the few small steps and quickly approached his friend with a wide smile. Appropriately, Gawain went down on one knee and bowed his head to the king. Uther turned to one of the ladies at his side and was given a beautifully woven crown of fragrant, spring flowers. They had clearly recently bloomed under the rapidly warming sun and beneath the soft showers of spring rain.

As Uther extended the wreath toward Gawain's head, the many spectators that had packed into the arena cheered their approval. They whistled and laughed and beamed at their most favorite knight emerging victorious once again. Gawain wasn't sure if the heat he felt in his ears was still a residual effect from the helmet he had just pulled off, or from this glorious reception.

"Well done, Sir Gawain," said Uther as he placed the wreath of flowers onto Gawain's head, "Although, if I'm being honest, I would've expected you to win this a little more handily."

Gawain simply grinned and said, "It's early spring. I'm still warming up."

~   ~   ~

The time for celebrations and feats of skill in the arena could only last so long. Gawain had done his part to keep up appearances, but now he had to get down to work. Despite his wins in the various tournaments and games, Gawain's upcoming rematch with the Green Knight pulled at the back of his mind. Sure, it was still nearly a year away, but Gawain wasn't the kind of man to put things off. Generally, he preferred to face his problems head on and charge right into them at full speed. His first challenge, however, was that he still didn't know where he was going to find the Green Knight when the year and a day was up. And so Gawain, who was mighty and unyielding in the fields of battle, ventured into a realm that wasn't so familiar to him.

The library.

The castle library was dominated by towering shelves all filled with dozens, if not hundreds, of enormous leather-bound books. Its collection had built up over many generations thanks to the handiwork of scores of travelling monks who had come to Tintagel and stayed for a few seasons or a few years and left thick copies of ancient volumes in return for food and lodging.

Most afternoons, Gawain found himself sneaking into the mostly vacant room of books. He always looked carefully around to make sure no one was watching him. He didn't want people to know how seriously he was taking this whole business. Once inside, he would scan the room to confirm no one was taking particular notice of him, and that he wasn't becoming too familiar with anyone else who was there. Then he would carefully select several thick dusty tomes and continue his research.

Very quickly, however, Gawain realized he had a very serious problem ahead of him. He knew next to nothing about the Green Knight. The strange emerald warrior hadn't given a real name. He hadn't mentioned anything about his realm. His armor and weapons were unusual and foreign, but didn't have any distinct features to work off of. Gawain had almost nothing to draw from. He was in the unfortunate position of having to grab books at random and slowly work his way through them with the hope that sooner or later he would stumble upon some mention of the Green Knight.

So far his hopes had not paid off.

Nonetheless, Gawain wasn't the type of man to give up on his duties. So he drew several large books off of the shelves each day . They always had promising titles like:

NOTORIOUS KNIGHTS OF THE REALM

MYSTICAL KINGDOMS OF LEGEND

DARKEST FOES AND WHERE TO FIND THEM

And Gawain always plopped them down onto an oak table near a window. Then he would settle into one of the library's most comfortable chairs which really wasn't very comfortable at all. And he would start to flip through the pages.

Just outside the window, an old oak tree had stood for nearly a hundred years. As the bright spring sun shone, the oak tree sprouted new tiny green buds.

Gawain kept flipping through the pages.

Weeks passed and the tree's lush green leaves spread out and flattened.

Gawain was still flipping.

It had been months and the leaves even started to crisp and dry around the edges.

And Gawain slammed the book he was reading shut. He had been through piles and piles of them. His eyes were starting to go cross-eyed from all the reading. If he never had to smell the polished leather of a book's binding again it would be too soon. At certain desperate times, Gawain was starting to wonder if the Green Knight even existed at all. Then in the middle of the night, Gawain would wake covered in sweat with a terrible knot in his stomach and remember that the Green Knight was only too real. And he was waiting for Gawain.

But Gawain had no idea how to find him.

~ ~ ~

CHAPTER 5

Dents in the Armor

In the heat of the summer, the bright sun stood high in the clear blue skies. The knight's arena was packed with just as many spectators as ever, and they fanned themselves with pieces of paper or their own hands if it came to that. It was a particularly sweltering day, and a brief shower of rain had only served to make the air thicker and more stifling. But no one was willing to miss the latest display by the great Sir Gawain.

The center of the slightly oval arena now bore a long railing and on either side were two knights atop their horses preparing for the most noble and exciting of exploits.

Jousting.

On his end, Gawain sat upon his faithful, slightly speckled gray horse. Ringolet had been with Gawain ever since he was officially knighted. The new knight and his horse learned together. Whenever Gawain had to go on a long journey it had been Ringolet that went with him.

Gawain pulled his helmet on, and an attendant placed the long lance into his right hand which Gawain hefted and raised high in the air. The crowd roared for him. With his left hand, Gawain patted the horse's neck.

"All right, Ringolet," Gawain said as he petted the mane, "Ready to show them how it's done?"

Ringolet neighed loudly and proudly. Gawain took it to definitively mean, "Oh, Yes!"

A straight-backed woman clutching a color handkerchief stood in the center of the ring. She looked to the challenger. He nodded to her that he was ready. Then she turned and looked in Gawain's direction. He too nodded. He was always ready. He lived for this. He couldn't wait to get going. The woman dropped the handkerchief and darted away.

They were off.

Gawain and Ringolet galloped forward, as the other lancer and his horse charged from the other direction. They each closed the distance with a burst of speed. Then they levelled their lances at one another.

Closer.... Closer... Closer.. Closer.

CRASH!

Both lances struck and erupted into clouds of tiny splinters.

And Gawain was knocked off his horse!

The crowd gasped in astonishment. Men's eyes went wide in shock. Their hero had been unhorsed! Women turned slightly pale as their jaws dropped. Their heart's secret desire had been beaten! Young children actually began to cry. The man that they all hoped to be like one day had been conquered!

From the dirt, Gawain rolled over painfully, and struggled to his knees. He gasped for breath and drew in ragged lungfuls of air as he ripped off his helmet. Several aides rushed to his side, but he waved them away. Unable to face the disappointed people, Gawain avoided looking into the stands. Instead, he looked across the arena to the king's wooden platform and found the throne.

Uther stared at him with worry and shock all over his regal face.

~ ~ ~

Gingerly hobbling just a bit, Gawain led Ringolet into the castle stables. Every breath he took still gave him a painful stab in the side, but Gawain gritted his teeth and hid it from everyone that he had encountered that afternoon after his embarrassing defeat. Instead, Gawain had laughed it all off. He had pretended it was of completely no consequence, and brushed it all away with a never ending stream of reasonable explanations.

"Everyone has a bad day every now and then."

"My opponent was very skilled and has a bright future ahead of him."

"I think I just ate something funny for breakfast."

Gawain's rosy attitude and seemingly unabashed acceptance of the ordeal quickly calmed down all of his fans. In no time at all, he waved them all away with a smile and a hearty laugh.

But now that he was removing Ringolet's bridle and brushing the horse's mane, Gawain couldn't help himself anymore as he exploded,

"You want to tell me what happened out there?!"

Ringolet wasn't the type of horse to accept an accusation like that, and he snuffled indignantly.

"Don't blame it on me!" shouted Gawain. "We've never lost a joust before. We've held that record for years now! I was counting on you."

The horse clearly had enough of Gawain's outbursts as he jerked his long head away from the brush that he normally enjoyed so much.

"Oho! Don't get angry at me! You're the one who didn't hold up your end of the bargain," said Gawain to the horse.

Once again, Ringolet huffed. He backed away into a small corner of the stable, and turned his massive rump in the direction of his master.

"I didn't lose my nerve!" the knight said. "I wouldn't have- If anyone did- All right! You're right! It's not all your fault. It's not your fault at all..."

Gawain's gaze dropped and the horse turned his large brown eyes back around to face his master. Finally, he stepped back up to meet Gawain. Ringolet turned his head ever so slightly and allowed Gawain to start brushing him again, which Gawain was only too happy to do. After a few moments of silence, however, Gawain looked around to make sure no one else was in the stables. Then he dropped his voice and said quietly,

"Can I be honest with you, Ringolet?"

The horse blinked his assent.

"I think... I may have made a mistake. I'm nervous about this one..."

Just saying the words made Gawain feel ashamed. He was the mighty knight whose exploits had been spread far and wide. Hadn't he overcome much greater challenges than this? What had he to be nervous about? He could do this. He could do it, right? The more he thought about it, the more Gawain realized that this was a challenge unlike any other that he had faced. Every other beast had been a menace and Gawain had rode in courageously to conquer it for the good of others. But this situation with the Green Knight could've been avoided. He had caused it with his own foolish pride. Now he had to get himself out of it. And as a rare hot wetness bit at the corners of his eyes, Gawain suddenly wasn't so sure he could overcome this one.

Ringolet leaned his head forward and nuzzled Gawain. And Gawain breathed easier.

"Eh, you're right," said Gawain as he patted Ringolet on the nose, "At least, I'll have you with me. And I'm still the greatest knight in the kingdom, aren't I?"

Ringolet neighed for him.

"It'll be a great adventure. A great adventure..."

~ ~ ~

CHAPTER 6

The Fall Approaches

The leaves on the old oak tree had started to turn various shades of orange, red and gold when Gawain finally gave up in the library. He had been through hundreds of books and had only been able to find brief mentions of the Green Knight. Mostly it had just been whispers about far away lands where the waters had run dry, the fields had gone barren, and the animals had turned beastly. None of it was particularly pleasant. And it had all been attributed to an unnaturally green-glowing warlord.

Unfortunately, none of them had mentioned the Green Knight's likely whereabouts.

Gawain was starting to worry that his task was hopeless. Not only was he having trouble tracking down the Green Knight's realm, but even if he did find it, what hope did Gawain have of being able to win the rematch? From what Gawain could find, the Green Knight was a foe unlike any he had ever faced before. The seven-foot tall, monstrous emerald knight had survived stabbings through the heart. He had walked away from thousand foot drops from towering cliffs. And Gawain had personally seen him pick up his own head off of the ground.

It seemed as if Gawain truly had made a deal with the devil and everyone and everything he held dear might suffer for his foolish pride.

More and more often, Gawain would take long walks through the countryside in order to clear his increasingly muddled head. He found that the chill autumn breeze helped to calm his nerves. However, the rapidly shortening days served as a reminder that his year was quickly coming to a close.

One hazy afternoon, Gawain found himself wandering into a small, meager village on the outskirts of the land that fell under Tintagel's protection. Oftentimes, he found himself preferring these remote, nearly deserted places. It was less likely for him to run into anyone here that would recognize him. Not long ago, he loved running into his adoring fans so that he might regale them with various stories of his greatness. But that all seemed like a lifetime ago. He didn't feel heroic anymore. Instead, he felt as if he was in a daze as he walked alone, lost in his own thoughts. A chill breeze blew by, scattering some dead leaves across his path, and also carried the distant jeering voices of a pack of young ruffians. Gawain's ears pricked up as he heard the taunts,

"Soured Coward, if you please,
Go get lost among the trees.
Never heard and never seen,
Go be taken by the green."

Then he heard the distinctive sound he knew so well of fists slamming into soft flesh, and soft cries of pain. He might've been a bit low lately, but Gawain was still a noble knight and he still took seriously his charge to help the downtrodden. He sprung to attention and his eyes searched the village for the source of the voices. About a hundred yards away, he spotted a gang of five boys, all about twelve or thirteen years old. They had all circled around a sixth slimmer boy and the bullies shoved and punched the boy as he did his best to stand strong against them.

"Oy! Stop that!" shouted Gawain as he sprinted over toward the gang of bullies.

As he got closer, Gawain heard them calling,

"Scaredy baby, please go forth,

Far away and to the north.

In the ruins, cold and mean,

Go be taken by the green."

Gawain finally caught up, grabbed the largest bully by the scruff, and nearly lifted him completely off the ground.

"Who do you think you are?!" demanded Gawain as he tossed the bully aside. "Outnumbering someone smaller than you?!"

With an easy toss and a swing of his arms, Gawain scattered the bullies who took off running even as they turned to laugh and hiss at the slim boy that had just come under Gawain's protection.

"You all right, boy?" asked Gawain.

The boy avoided Gawain's eye contact as he clearly struggled to blink back tears.

"Don't worry. They're gone now," said Gawain as he clapped the boy on the shoulder. "They hurt you?"

The boy shook his head as he stared at the dirt and doggedly avoided Gawain's eyes. For his part, Gawain understood the delicate situation the boy was in, and understood that the boy still couldn't speak without risking hot tears spilling down his cheeks.

"Bunch of wretches. Attacking in a gang. Shouting rhymes like-" and Gawain's voice fell silent as a thought occurred to him. Suddenly, he demanded of the boy, "What were they saying to you?"

The boy cleared his throat, and his voice finally came out a little shaky, but he was doing well at hiding the slight catch in it.

"They-they called me a coward," said the boy, "Because I wouldn't throw stones at an old cat."

"Yes, but... what was that rhyme?" asked Gawain. It was clear the boy was embarrassed, but Gawain insistently waved him on, "Go ahead, boy, I need to know."

Refusing to meet Gawain's eyes, the boy reluctantly recited the schoolyard taunt,

"Scaredy baby, please go forth,

Far away and to the north.

In the ruins, cold and mean,

Go be taken by the green."

Gawain frowned as he took in the words and asked, "What does that mean? 'Go be taken by the green?'"

"It's just a tease," said the boy, and Gawain noted with pride that there was growing defiance in the young voice. It was clear that this boy was going to be all right after all, and he continued in a strong voice, "There's supposed to a monstrous man of green that takes away cowards-"

"'Far away and to the north,'" said Gawain completing the boy's thought.

"I guess..."

But Gawain's mind was already darting ahead as he recited the next line, "'In the ruins, Cold and mean...'"

His feet caught up with his racing mind and Gawain took off running for the castle. He was already twenty feet away when he remembered that he had left the boy in the lurch. Pausing for a moment, Gawain turned back to shout,

"By the way, lad, if they come back, hit them right here-"

And Gawain pointed to his sternum. Gawain mimicked a quick, hard jab right to the center of the chest.

"Throw all your weight into it. Hit them as hard as you can right in the middle of the chest. It'll stop their heart just for an instant. Even the biggest man will go right to sleep. That'll quiet them for good."

Then Gawain turned and sprinted away, but not without catching a quick, determined glance on the boy's face as he mimicked the strike to the chest of his imaginary assailants. Gawain grinned and felt a warm flush of pride as he became sure that the boy wouldn't be picked on again anytime soon.

~ ~ ~

The castle's library was completely deserted when Gawain burst in. Most of the torches had burned down, and Gawain had to squint against the darkness as he scoured through the tall bookcases. His eyes raked across the shelves of old leather tomes with their faded writing until he finally found the one he sought. Gawain pulled down a particularly ominous looking volume that was decorated with ancient, archaic symbols. He slammed it down on the table and began to read:

LOST CIVILIZATIONS TO THE NORTH

~ ~ ~

CHAPTER 7
All Hallow's Eve

Ghosts, ghouls and witches were swarming through the feasting hall as it played host to a grand and elaborate masquerade party. The stain glass window had been repaired months ago and now depicted Sir Lionel the Lion-hearted lancing a lion. The many statues throughout the hall had been decorated with dripping candles and other worldly adornments. Fair lords and gentle ladies were all dressed in colorful costumes, extravagant ball gowns, or garish attire. Lively music pulsed through the massive room and scores of people danced exuberantly.

For the occasion, Gawain was dressed much like his normal self, but taken to a further extreme. His hair and beard were adorned with even more trinkets, amulets and talismans. A golden-colored phoenix feather hung off the tip of one braided tendril. His face was painted with interlocking runes that had been taught to him by a hundred and fifty year old gypsy who Gawain had stumbled upon during his first journey to the distant deserts. His clothes were colorful and exotic as they had been scrapped together from gifts and treasures he had accumulated in all his worldly travels.

And he was using it all to impress a lovely lady made up to look like a tigress.

"When I came upon the Lady of the Fountain she was in a state of undress, of course," whispered Gawain into the lovely lady's ear, and he was pleased to hear her purr appropriately. "But she wasn't bashful about it. In fact, she encouraged me to join her. Which I felt obliged to do."

The lady dressed as a tigress meowed just at the thought of it. Gawain grinned and leaned in so close that he could feel her warm breath against his skin. He was about to kiss her-

When he caught a flash of green.

Suddenly all the joy drained from Gawain's face. He scanned through the crowd and spotted the backside of a man dressed all in green. Panic set in. Gawain recognized the double-headed ax. The Green Knight was here?! Without a word, he left the tigress's side and she hissed at his sudden rudeness. But Gawain couldn't have cared less as he thrust his way into the crowd.

Gawain's heart pounded as he hunted for his quarry through the throngs of partiers. Colors and costumes blurred together, but Gawain doggedly pursued the backside of the Green Knight. He shoved outraged dancers aside as he tried desperately to catch up. Finally, he saw the great double-headed ax on the Green Knight's back. Gawain lunged forward and caught the Green Knight by the shoulder. Gawain spun him around and clutched the green robes in his clenched fists.

"Are you taunting me?!" roared Gawain. "How dare you come back here?! I'll cut you down again right now!"

"Sir Gawain, stop!"

The harsh command made Gawain freeze and compose himself. He slackened his grip and turned to see King Uther Pendragon surveying him with a stern glance that clearly said, What is wrong with you?

Gawain looked around and realized that the entire celebration had come to a halt, and all of the guests were looking at him with similar expressions of worry and confusion. All eyes were on Gawain. And he finally took a good look at the man in his clutches. He was just an ordinary man in a green costume. He wasn't even a particularly big or impressive man.

And the ax on his back looked downright fake.

Gawain let the slightly trembling man go, and muttered a barely audible apology. The man in the green knight costume couldn't scurry away fast enough. For his part, Gawain shook his head furiously at his own mistake. How could he have let himself act like that?

In a moment, Uther was at Gawain's side and placed a reassuring hand on his friend's shoulder.

"I'm sorry. I don't know what came over me," said Gawain and his apology to the king was only slightly more intelligible than the one he had just given to the man he had accosted.

But Uther simply turned to the crowd, smiled, and ordered in his clear ringing voice, "Start the music again! Come now, everyone. Enjoy the celebration!"

At the king's order, the music started once more, and the many guests in their many costumes resumed their many revelries. Uther put his arm around Gawain and they watched the crowds form once more as people quickly forgot what all the commotion was all about. They each spotted the man in the green knight costume, and then with a lurch of disgust, Gawain noticed that it wasn't only one. There were a handful of men who had similarly chosen to dress as the green knight complete with painted axes strapped upon their backs.

"Costumes..." stated Uther with a hint that he shared in Gawain's disgust, "It doesn't take long for people to forget about how serious business actually begins, does it?"

"I'm sorry, my king," said Gawain more clearly this time.

Gawain bowed his head in supplication, but Uther waved his hand and gestured for Gawain to straighten up.

"Stand up," said Uther. "Come now, you don't need to bow to me. But I do humbly ask that you walk beside me, my friend."

Following in the king's footsteps, Gawain worked his way through the crowd of people. He had caught his breath and calmed down, but his face still felt flush as cold sweat trickled down his forehead and smeared the delicately drawn facade of paint he had created upon his knightly features. Gawain watched as people joked, laughed, and celebrated. He wished that he could join them, but he couldn't shake the pit from his stomach.

Uther Pendragon opened a door, and they emerged out onto a stone balcony just off of the feasting hall. The cool night air freed up Gawain from his anxieties and he gulped in deep rich breaths. He put his hands on the railing and hunched ever so slightly. Uther gazed up at the full moon and watched as silvery slivers of cloud crept in front of the massive floating orb.

"A full moon on All Hallow's Eve," remarked Uther. "It's a wonder we're not all losing our minds."

Gawain finally stood up straight as he shook his head, "I'm fine. Fine. Just too much to drink is all."

Enough was enough and Gawain had enough. He puffed out his chest impressively as he chose to stand tall and act like the great knight that he was. And he dared anyone to challenge his performance. He stood side-by-side with his king for several long moments and drank in the peaceful stillness of the night.

"I've heard you're preparing to leave," said Uther finally, "So soon? The year's not up yet."

"I've got a long journey ahead of me," was Gawain's reply.

"You've found him then?"

"What I've found is mostly whispers, but it should be enough to start on," admitted Gawain. "Ghost villages up north. Lunatics who can barely do anything but mutter, 'the Green Knight, the Green Knight, the Green Knight.' Over and over and over again. Exciting stuff..."

"It's not much to go on," said Uther.

"That's why I'm leaving early," shrugged Gawain as he felt a shiver that couldn't entirely be blamed upon the night air, "It'll still take some time to find the exact location of the Knight's Chapel. But I'll find him."

"You know, you don't have to go," said the good king warmly to his loyal knight.

"I made a promise," was the knight's gruff response.

Uther shook his head, "It wasn't exactly a fair wager. You were goaded and tricked. You don't owe him a rematch."

"He promised doom upon this land if I don't," said Gawain ominously. "From the mentions I've found of him, he can deliver."

"I don't believe that for an instant."

"If it is true, I couldn't live with myself if I was the cause of it."

"And I couldn't live with myself if I let you die."

Uther placed his hand on Gawain's shoulder once more, and Gawain felt that in that moment they weren't a king and his knight, they were friends. And he loved Uther for it. Nonetheless, Gawain shook his head. He had made up his mind long ago, and nothing, not his king, not even a friend, could stop him.

That didn't mean that Uther wouldn't try, though, and the king said, "Stay here, Sir Gawain. I fear for you, if you go. And I promise you that we shall all stand with you in your hour of need."

"That's very kind of you, my king," said Gawain. "But I'm a man of my word. And I must honor that."

"I'm not sure it's honor that's guiding you," said Uther as he resumed his regal wisdom. "Be careful of your pride, good Sir Gawain."

And with that, King Uther Pendragon patted his friend on the shoulder and left Gawain alone to watch as the bright, shining moon was slowly covered by a blanket of clouds that could block but not entirely cancel out its light.

~ ~ ~

The next morning's rays came much too quickly for Gawain. They began by sneaking over the distant hilltops, then they picked up speed as they rushed through the wide grasses of the plains. The golden sunshine then filled the nearby villages and awoke the chirping birds in their trees. Finally, it reached the castle's walls, crept through the single small window and into Gawain's sparse chambers. However, it didn't awaken Gawain. It couldn't. Because he had never slept. The mighty knight sat upright in his bed surrounded by his trophies and trinkets. His hair and beard were already adorned with the pagan amulets and foreign charms that he believed would bring him luck. Hours earlier, he had pulled on his armor painted with ancient runes and little known spells that promised to keep him safe.

As the day's light flooded into his room, Gawain rose from his bed, stretched his back, shook out his limbs, and set off for his journey. Fortunately, his first stop would be his easiest.

He had to meet his most loyal friend.

Gawain found Ringolet ready and waiting in the stables, and Gawain was warmed by the sight of his good and noble horse. He took his time preparing Ringolet by weaving shiny talismans and wooden amulets into the horse's long mane and tail. Then Gawain fitted Ringolet with his polished saddle and filled them with supplies as they prepared for the adventures that lay ahead.

"It'll be an adventure," said the knight to his horse. "One that they'll very probably write poems about. Great epic poems with rhyming couplets. 'Sir Gawain and his Great Horse.' That'll be the title, you'll see!"

Ringolet snuffled at Gawain, and Gawain lurched in shock.

"No, you can't have your name first!"

~   ~   ~

At his most peaceful spot, high atop the tallest tower in Tintagel Castle, King Uther Pendragon had been up since before sunrise. He had watched the bright golden sun climbing high into the skies turning it from blustery tones of gray into smooth oceans of blue. He had listened to the early morning songs of the few birds who had chosen not to fly away from the winter's chill. He had felt the brisk invigorating breeze as it danced across his cheeks and bit at his ears.

But there was no peace in Uther's heart this morning.

A short time after the sun had risen, Uther had looked to the eastern corner of his castle. The wind seldom blew in from that direction so it had been the perfect place to have the royal stables built. His own horse lived there as did the horses of all his closest advisors, confidants, and knights. It was the place where Sir Gawain kept his noble steed, Ringolet.

As the sun rose ever higher into the sky, King Uther Pendragon watched his good friend and his loyal horse ride out of the stables and set out to tempt their fates. Deep within his bones, the king rippled with a deep sadness, because he was eerily certain that he would never see Gawain again.

And he was right.

~   ~   ~

CHAPTER 8

Men, Mermaids, and Monasteries

Upon leaving the stables at Tintagel, Gawain almost immediately began to feel like his old self again. He had been so riled up over the past several months, and yet, he had no place to put his energies. However, now that he galloped away with his faithful steed, Gawain finally felt himself filling with that familiar sense of adventure. He relished the quest that lay ahead of him, and his heart filled with excitement.

The only problem was that he still wasn't sure where he was headed.

In all of his many hours in the castle library, Gawain had only come across fleeting mentions of the spectral Green Knight who overtook proud men's kingdoms and turned their lands against them. There were only two things that Gawain had learned for certain. First, the Green Knight hailed from the cold lands far to the north. Second, he tended to target strong, powerful men. Based on that information alone, Gawain had at least a notion of where to start.

The Roman general Sagramore had built up a reputation as one the greatest conquerors in the empire. He had led his troops to incredible victories over rampaging barbarians. He had held the resistance in outmatched Roman strongholds despite overwhelming numbers of invading pirates. He miraculously managed to ward off a herd of angry centaurs that were still upset over the unlicensed use of their likeness in the sacking of Troy, even though ironically that was what led to the creation of Rome in the first place. In the waning days of Rome's immense empire, Sagramore was considered a shining beacon of hope and strength for the masses.

And then one day, at the height of his success, he threw down his sword to become a farmer.

Knowing that he could never live a simple life of a commoner in Rome, Sagramore journeyed to the lands of Briton to begin his new quiet life. However, he couldn't escape the occasional unwanted guest, and as Gawain galloped over the gentle slopes of Sagramore's farm, the old Roman glowered in the direction of the rugged knight.

"Hello there, Sagramore!" called Gawain.

Sagramore simply glared, but his glare unmistakably said, *Gawain...*

During his days as a Roman commander, Sagramore had believed that speaking too much made a man weak, and so he had meticulously trained himself to only utter the most essential of orders. As time passed, and as he became a more and more accomplished leader, Sagramore perfected his use of pointed glances and stern gazes. It was astonishing what the man could convey with a simple look.

"It's good to see you, my friend!" said Gawain as he slowed his horse to a trot and dismounted to stand beside Sagramore. "How long's it been? 10 years? Longer?"

Sagramore just stared in a way that said, *What do you want from me, Gawain?*

"All right, all right, I'll get to the point," said Gawain. "I just thought a few pleasantries might be in order after all these years. But I see you're as unflappable as ever, so I'll get on with it. I'm seeking a knight for a duel. Stands over seven feet tall. Prefers to battle with an ax. Oh, and he glows green from head to toe."

Sagramore narrowed his eyelids ever so slightly as if to say, *I know him.*

"I knew you would!" said Gawain as he flushed with encouragement. "This Green Knight prefers to challenge the strongest of men. I figured he couldn't have resisted coming after a man of your reputation. And judging by the pitiful state of your farm here, I guess he got the better of you."

The glare that came from Sagramore made Gawain immediately realize that he had misspoken.

"I mean, of course, you didn't fall for his tricks!" stammered Gawain under the intensity of Sagramore's stare. "And there's clearly nothing wrong with your farm! In fact, it looks like it's flourishing nicely. Ah yes, I can see some nice carrots, and turnips, and… uh… roots… or rocks or some such…"

Sagramore gritted his jaw as if to say, *Get on with it, Gawain.*

Gawain jumped at the chance to continue, "Anyway, I was hoping you might point me in the right direction."

After a deep frustrated sigh from the Roman, Gawain was fixed with a stare that clearly said, *The Green Knight challenged me to a duel, but of course, I wasn't foolish enough to accept the offer. No matter how many insults and boasts he threw at me, I remained unmoved. He left disappointed and rode to the north. I know not where. But I've heard rumors that the harbors of Anglesey befell terrible tidings. The fish disappeared and the waters turned violent causing the men to abandon the villages. You might learn something there.*

Gawain marvelled at what Sagramore could convey with a look and he said, "Anglesey. Thank you, my friend. I'll look there next."

Knowing that he was unlikely to be invited in for tea, Gawain was about to remount Ringolet when Sagramore cleared his throat softly and said with a slight shake of his head,

I thought you knew better than this, Gawain...

This gave Gawain a moment's pause, but he too shook his head and forced a laugh as he said, "Please, I'm the mighty Sir Gawain! The greatest knight to ever serve the mighty Uther Pendragon. And the world will be better off when I quickly and easily dispatch that great green menace. Don't you worry about me. I know what I'm doing."

The look on Sagramore's face showed that he was far from convinced.

Gawain got back atop Ringolet, but before he dug his heels in to canter off, he asked, "So how are you liking the life of a farmer?"

Sagramore's face fell as he sighed and spoke aloud,
"I thought being a Roman general was hard..."

~ ~ ~

In the past, Gawain had always enjoyed visiting the sea towns that ran along the isles of Anglesey. The fresh ocean air had always helped him to breathe a little easier. The fisherman were always good for a lively tale featuring sharks and giant squids. And they were the only men alive who could compete with Gawain for the title of fullest, most manly beard.

But things had changed in the many years since Gawain had last stopped by.

The ports which had once been bustling and noisy were now deserted. A few ghostly abandoned ships rocked placidly upon the waves as they were held in place by sturdy, old, moss covered ropes. But there wasn't a soul in sight. Gawain tied up Ringolet and warily walked along the moldy wooden piers to investigate. He wasn't destined to find much. The place was completely empty, and what might have been left behind seemed to have been washed away by the sea long ago. After searching for over an hour, Gawain stomped back along the platform and was prepared to leave empty-handed when he heard a husky woman's call.

"Oooooh, be that Gawain I lay eyes upon?" cooed the feminine voice.

"Fill up me heart with thy knight's song!" said another.

Gawain turned and looked back to the water just as a small pod of mermaids emerged from the dark surface of the sea. He grinned.

Gawain had always nursed a soft spot for mermaids. Sure, their hair was matted and waxy like a seal's, but that was necessary for them to maintain some oil in the cold waters. And yes, their breath always stunk of raw fish, but again they were creatures of the sea, it wasn't like they could start a fire to cook their meals. What Gawain liked best, however, was their generous stores of soft blubber that made them round and inviting and deliciously warm. Gawain always imagined that one day, when all his journeys were through, he might wrap his strong arms around a plump mermaid and allow himself to be blissfully lost to the sea.

"Why hello there, ladies," called Gawain with a bow of his head. He quickly counted five of the sea women, but Orgeluse, the most robust of them, quickly swam closest.

"Do my senses deceive me?" the mermaid asked. "Sir Gawain, the waters have washed round the world and back since last we met."

"Aye, it's been at least seven years by my count, and I've been the worse off for it," said Gawain as he winked at the mermaids. "I've missed those big warm welcoming arms of yours, Orgeluse."

"Dive your weary bones right in then?"

The mermaid seductively beckoned Gawain with a webbed finger.

"Believe me, I am tempted," said Gawain. "But I'm afraid I've got to keep my feet on land for now. You see, I'm on a quest. Got a score to settle. With a nasty fellow bearing a green glow about him. Know anything about it?"

All five mermaids exchanged glances and Gawain got the feeling that they weren't pleasant.

"Better off with us, you'd be," Orgeluse said with a slight gurgling coo.

"So you do know about him?"

Orgeluse dipped her face just below the water and sighed causing large bubbles to rise on the surface of the water and break, then she rose and said, "A bit up the coast, there be strange happenings with the beasts beneath the shoals. Sharks with green eyes turnin' mad. Seals glowing green and battlin' with one another without so much as a fish to fight over. And every story, every dark occurrence, comes back to the stupidity of a single man. The greatest fisherman on the peninsula, he was said to be. Until he lost a spear throwin' contest to this knight with your green disposition."

Gawain's heart sank, but Orgeluse bobbed up as she continued.

"Turned all the seas around here against 'im. The poor fisherman, once so proud, but always so foolish, lost everything. Don't let his past, be a glimpse of your future, Gawain. The Green Knight gives me a shiver, and I can stay warm most any the current."

Gawain once again took in Orgeluse's warm, luxurious plumpness and wished he could forget about his quest. But he'd come too far now, and even though he knew he had a long way yet to go, he was ready for the journey and prepared for the fight.

"Any idea where I can find him?"

"Word flows quickly hear amongst the waters. The fish and squids talk about strange doings up in Wirral. The sharks point to Holywell. The sensible ones just stay away."

"They're in the same direction," said Gawain. "I guess, that's where I'll head next."

"We mermaids beg you again, Gawain," came Orgeluse's insistent call. "Stay with us. Float above all this. Dive on past it. We'll swim to the warm sweet waters down to the south. We'll take good care of you. I doubt that your dueling partner will do the same."

"Can't do that, my lady, I've got too much on the line," said Gawain as he shook his head and forced a light tone in his voice. "But don't worry your pretty, seaweed-covered locks over me. I plan to keep my head safely above water."

~ ~ ~

And so, Gawain's journey continued.

Yet in stop after stop, he found the same thing. Every mention of the Green Knight was always accompanied by tales of despair and ruin. Gawain sought out remote cabins in the woods, only to find them overrun by beasts. He sailed to deserted islands, and found them crumbling into the sea. He even visited a burnt down old kitchen, only to be told of a strange incident where a boastful baker lost a pie cooking contest and had paid a terrible price. Each destination provided a clue to Gawain as to where he might search next, but none of them seemed helpful in identifying Gawain's final location, the home of the Green Knight himself, where Gawain's rematch loomed and looked increasingly hopeless.

And so the journey continued.

In the wild lands of Wirral, Gawain learned of a peaceful clan of druids who had all been cut down by the Green Knight. They had made the forests their home for over a century and learned ancient secrets of healing through their connection to the trees. However, one of their leaders had been seduced into a deadly contest of bow staffs, and the whole clan had been held responsible when he was inevitably defeated. There were rumors that maybe one or two of their young women had made it out alive, but vague whispers did Gawain no good. Instead, he and Ringolet found themselves fighting their way out of the wilds when a pack of roaming beasts turned on them.

And so the journey continued.

At the Holywell Abbey, Gawain found a small group of nuns. They told a tale of a monastery hidden amongst the hills where one foolish monk was fooled into giving up his vow of silence. A drinking contest ensued which the monk, of course, lost. Within months, the entire remote holy place was crumbling and destroyed. Gawain, who had a deep affection for a good drink himself, grimaced at the thought that not even monks were immune to the Green Knight's entreaties. It was with the nuns, however, that Gawain finally found a ray of hope. The women said that before the monastery had collapsed they had heard of the destruction of a fortress far to the north. Pulford was supposed to be invulnerable, but now it lay in ruin. The story went that the poor ruined fortress was the first place to fall to the Green Knight, meaning that it might provide the key to finally finding that terrible emerald warrior.

And Gawain finally had a sign that his journey might be nearing its end.

~   ~   ~

CHAPTER 9

The Sad Fate of Pulford Fortress

The stronghold at Pulford had once stood as one of the most secure and impressive fortresses on the northern peninsula. Gawain had never visited there before, but in his youth, he had heard many stories about the thrilling defenses it had mounted against invading hordes of Vikings, barbarians, and abominable snow monsters.

It didn't look so good anymore.

Sitting atop Ringolet, Gawain slowly trotted through the gray desolate landscape. The ground had become rocky and barren and looked like it hadn't grown anything in years. Every tree that they passed was gnarled and dead, seemingly just waiting for the right gust of wind to finally topple them and put them out of the their misery. The sky was bleak and colorless with cold winds whipping about as a few flurried snowflakes floated lifelessly on the air. There was an unnaturally heavy fog that seemed to obscure the castle, and Gawain was surprised to suddenly find himself nearly upon it as he passed large scattered hunks of rock that were once part of the walls.

Suddenly, the fog blew aside for an instant and Gawain got his first look at the castle lying in utter ruin.

Gawain shuddered as he dismounted and warily approached the fallen fortress. He led Ringolet by the reins and they closed in on what seemed the be the largest intact portion of the castle. It was a tall ragged wall that never reached a ceiling. Nonetheless, Gawain followed along the length of the wall until he found an old rotting wooden door with rusted metal hinges leading...

Somewhere.

With a deep sigh, Gawain reached for the door handle. Then he paused, and he looked to Ringolet.

"You stay here."

Almost a little too quickly, Ringolet neighed in assent. Gawain stared in disbelief at the horse.

"You great, four-legged baby!"

The horse huffed back at him.

"I am going! I'm not afraid! It's just an empty, deserted, crumbling unconquerable castle. What's there to be afraid of?"

Then with a glare at his horse, Gawain opened the door, and entered the ruins.

Somewhat to his relief, the door didn't close easily behind him, and Gawain was happy to leave it wide open as he took the first steps down a dark crumbling staircase. It looked as if he was the first one to use these stone steps in quite some time. Or the first man at least. There were plenty of rats that seemed to scuttle and dart into porous dripping corners. And there didn't seem to be any shortage of spiders either. Gawain brushed down thick, white cobwebs and fat, black spiders scurried away. He carefully tread down the slippery flight of steps and was surprised to see how deep it went. He turned and looked back up toward the door and realized that if he was going to continue he would need more light than the meager opening would provide. Gawain took an old torch out of its bracket on the wall. From his belt he drew out some flint, and struck it. He was relieved to find that at least the torch still had some life left in it.

Gawain held the now crackling torch aloft as he continued down into the depths of this once mighty castle.

Deeper.

Deeper.

More rat infested.

Deeper.

Finally, Gawain came to another old door, and the mighty knight wrenched it open to find a dungeon that looked like something he had seen in his nightmares. Water seeped in through its crumbling ceiling. Scores of rusted metal shackles protruded from the walls and lay strewn about the floor like great snakes just preparing to strike.

And in one corner was a skeleton.

These were the times when Gawain was grateful for being so unquestionably brave. Ignoring the pit in his stomach, Gawain walked over to the pile of bones and examined the tattered robes, and found clutched in the dead man's hands an old dust-covered leather book. Gawain sighed and reminded himself that this man had probably read this book enough times, then Gawain ripped it out of the dead man's grasp with a sickening crunch. In all of his many researches back in Tintagel's library, Gawain had come to learn that when it came to the tales of ghost castles it was best to skip to the end, so he flipped to the last page and found a final scrawled entry that read:

I FEAR THE DUNGEON WON'T KEEP ME SAFE MUCH LONGER. HE'S COMING. UNSTOPPABLE. UNTIRING. HE SURVIVED MY BLOW THROUGH HIS HEART. NOW HE HAS CONSUMED MY LANDS. CRUSHED MY CASTLE. DECIMATED MY FOLLOWERS. I WISH I HAD NEVER AGREED TO HIS DEVIL'S DUEL. I WISH I HAD MET HIM IN HIS CHAPEL IN OLD SWYTHAMLEY. PERHAPS HE WOULD'VE SPARED MY PEOPLE. MY GOD... WHAT HAVE I DONE?

Gawain lowered the book and looked at the skeleton. Gawain felt a lurch in his stomach as he vowed that, no matter what happened to him in the coming days, he would face his fate. He wouldn't end up like this cursed man. And, with the merest feeling of relief, Gawain recognized that he now finally knew where he was headed.

"Old Swythamley..."

Gawain grumbled in disgust.

~   ~   ~

CHAPTER 10
The Lady and the Wolves

Galloping through a desolate bit of forest, Gawain felt a deep chill through his bones that could only partially be attributed to the increasingly frosty air. He now felt confident that the direction he was headed was the right one, and yet he felt more lost than ever. Old Swythamley was a notorious valley that lay between two dark mountains. The rumor was that even the fiercest of beasts refused to go there, and those who were brave enough to make the journey never returned. In fact, in all his many travels and dealings, Gawain had never met a single creature who had been there, which only seemed to confirm the theory that once a person went in they never came back.

Gawain pulled up on Ringolet's reins, and the normally tireless horse came to halt to catch his breath. The two of them glanced around at the distinctly unfriendly territory. There were no shortage of trees, but not a bit of green or warmth to be seen. The branches reached out like spider legs gently creeping through the sky. The trunks creaked as the dry leafless trees bent softly under the relentless barrage of the cold wind. The groaning of the wood made Gawain think of legends he had heard of talking trees that bore the spirits of ancient sorcerers and malicious ghouls. Gawain couldn't wait to move on.

The brave knight looked around to get his bearings before they continued onward when a sharp cracking noise broke the silence. Without a moment's hesitation, Gawain drew his sword and prepared himself for battle against whatever minion of darkness hoped to ambush them.

It was just a rabbit. Just a simple fluffy rabbit.

Gawain chuckled, and patted Ringolet's neck.

"You're getting jumpy, old friend."

The horse grumbled in a passable imitation of his rider's favorite expression.

The rabbit bounded away in the direction that Gawain and Ringolet had just come from. Gawain was pleased with the fact that there was still some life in this increasingly bleak place. However, he was also disappointed to see that the little bit of life seemed to be rapidly deserting the land.

"I don't blame you," Gawain called to the loping rabbit, "I don't much want to be heading this way myself. I'm not sure what's there for us."

Almost as if in answer, a woman's shriek of terror tore through the gray air. Loud. Shrill. Clearly in mortal danger. It was exactly what a knight looked for in a day's work.

"Well, there's that," said Gawain before digging his heels into Ringolet's flanks.

In a flash, the horse took off at a gallop. At Gawain's urging, Ringolet beat through the bleak forest and his hooves thundered against the hard frozen soil. They streaked amongst the barren trees, and Gawain's eyes raked through the landscape until he finally saw the source of the scream far ahead in a valley spotted with sparse dry weeds.

A tall woman with long tresses of free-flowing dirty blonde hair and dressed in a simple ankle-length dress stood alone at the bottom of the valley.

Well, not exactly alone.

She was surrounded by a pack of wolves.

The blonde lady clutched a large tree branch and swung it desperately at the wolves. A quick count by Gawain ascertained that there were seven wolves. One branch didn't seem destined to hold them off for long.

Once again, Gawain snapped Ringolet's reins and they leapt forward even faster. Swifter and swifter they rode across the cold wasteland toward the blonde lady, seeking to be the mighty knight and the noble steed to the rescue. It was far from certain that they would make it in time. Gawain and Ringolet cut the distance, but the wolves were growing restless. Even from a distance, Gawain could hear their snarls and see their raised hackles and foaming mouths. The blonde lady swung her branch and impressively cracked one wolf that was getting too close for comfort. The other wolves, however, snapped and barked at her as they prepared to pounce.

Gawain pushed Ringolet on. C'mon... C'mon... C'mon...

The wolves dug their claws into the cold ground as they reared back to leap. Their mouths were open and ready to feast.

When Gawain finally arrived.

He leapt off of his horse, and he brandished his sword at the wolves who, he was relieved to find, were sufficiently interested in their own survival to fall back upon the knight's arrival. They were far from retreating, however, as they now turned their attention to the strong knight and the sturdy horse that they must've considered a much more attractive meal. Gawain was somewhat surprised that the pack of wolves didn't disperse, since he knew from years of hunting that ordinary wolves preferred easy prey. As Gawain faced them, though, he quickly realized that these weren't ordinary wolves. For one thing, they were slightly larger than the average variety and they had fuller, more muscular bodies as if they had no problem finding plentiful meals. Their gray coats were also thick and seemed to slightly bristle independently of the chill breeze.

Most ominous of all, their eyes glowed an otherworldly shade of emerald green.

"I guess you didn't housebreak them when they were puppies," said Gawain.

"You know, you miss feeding them one time…" the blonde lady replied and her voice sounded surprisingly calm and determined.

Brave and funny, thought Gawain. He liked that in a woman. He grinned as he held out his arms to shield the lady from the strange beasts. He was fairly certain that he could take on the entire pack, but it would be harder if he had to keep an eye on her too. So Gawain turned his head just enough to address his horse while still keeping his gaze locked on the wolves who seemed only to eager to get their feast underway.

"Ringolet, get her out of here!" commanded Gawain.

But the horse wasn't going anywhere as he stamped his front hooves at the foaming wolves and neighed at them furiously.

"Would you do what I tell you for once?!" said Gawain with exasperation, but also a hint of gratitude.

"I think he knows you'll need his help," said the lady as she crouched in an attack position and held the branch defensively. "And mine."

As if they knew that a real fight was shaping up, one of the wolves sprung forward, but Gawain slashed at it, drawing blood from its snout. It fell back looking more furious than ever. That seemed to go for the entire pack which was looking more and more blood-thirsty.

"No. I won't put a lady in danger," stated Gawain firmly.

"You didn't put me in danger. I put myself here," was her just-as-firm reply, "And I intend to help you get us both out of it."

Suddenly, she lunged forward to kiss Gawain on the cheek. It was just a peck, but it was the first real warmth he'd felt in weeks. It radiated all the way down into his fingers and toes, and the numb flesh of his cold cheek flushed where her soft lips had touched it.

"For luck," she said.

It did the trick. The mighty Gawain, the conqueror of all manner of man and beast, was ready for battle.

His smile didn't last for long, though, as the wolves sprang all at once. To protect the lady, Gawain thrust himself into the center of the pack, and quickly found himself surrounded by foaming, four-legged beasts. He spun and slashed at them as they bit and clawed at him from all sides, and for a while his flashing sword and mighty fists were enough to repel them. But he was vastly outnumbered and it was only a matter of time before one of them got their teeth on him.

"We need fire!" Gawain shouted as he tossed the lady his flint and striking stone. If she was determined to stay, Gawain figured he should put her to good use.

Another wolf pounced. Another slash from Gawain.

"The wood will never catch!" cried the lady.

Teeth. Pounce. Slash.

"If only there was some fabric somewhere you could spare..." said Gawain through gritted teeth as he batted away another vicious animal with his free left hand.

The lady got the hint, and Gawain was pleased to see that modesty didn't plague her mind in moments of danger, as she began to tear at the edge of her long dress. With long ripping motions, she pulled several long strips of extra fabric from the bottom few inches down near her ankles. As Gawain kicked at another wolf, he saw the lady wrapping the fabric around the end of her branch. Gawain allowed himself to breathe a sigh of relief, for in a moment, she would have a blazing torch and that would go a long way toward scattering the wolves. He'd just have to hold them off a little longer.

It was a nice thought, anyway.

Two wolves leapt at Gawain. He was able to slash one away, but the other sunk its teeth into his left forearm. The righteous knight screamed in pain in a way that he admitted was less than manly. The rest of the pack saw their opportunity and another wolf pounced upon him.

And another. And another. And another.

Their sharp teeth and vicious claws ripped into his flesh.

Vaguely, in the edge of his vision, Gawain saw the blonde lady sparking at the fabric. But it was no good. Not yet. And it was seemingly less and less likely that it would be in time. Gawain fell to his knees at the onslaught of the wolves.

Just keep getting up, thought Gawain as he struggled to regain his footing even as he saw another wolf about to pounce.

The snarling, green-eyed monsters were about to overtake Gawain when a larger, heavier beast lunged forward. Ringolet stomped into the fight and kicked two of the wolves. The rest of the pack scattered for a moment, and Gawain was reminded once again that he had truly chosen the right horse. Gawain finally got to his feet and resumed his battle with the wolves. Ringolet kicked another wolf, and as it fell to the ground, Gawain sprung forward and stabbed his sword downward into the heart of the beast. One wolf was not going to bother them anymore. Yet another wolf sprung at him instantly.

CRACK!

The springing wolf was struck by a the club of a tree branch.

"Who needs fire?" said the lady with shrug.

"I had it under control…" Gawain said, although his breathing was becoming heavy and ragged. "But thank you…"

Suddenly the fight had turned. Two wolves cowered at the new show of force, and Gawain struck at them. Two less wolves to worry about. Between the lady's club, Gawain's sword, and Ringolet's stomping hooves, the wolves didn't stand a chance. In a matter of minutes, the beasts all lay dead, and Gawain stood heaving and bloody in the cold night air.

"I can't thank you enough. If you hadn't come when you did…" began the lady, but she was quickly cut off by the pained gasps that came from the stumbling knight.

"That's what… a knight… is for…"

And Gawain collapsed and fell unconscious.

~ ~ ~

CHAPTER 11
Hautdesert Castle

With a painful twinge in his arm, Gawain groggily awoke and was surprised to find himself in a soft bed with his armor stripped away. He struggled to sit up and every movement shot some kind of piercing pain through some part of his body. But he was used to pain, it came with the job, and he forced himself into a sitting position anyway so that he could take stock of his unusual surroundings. The bedroom wasn't much bigger than his chambers back at Tintagel unless, of course, he counted the huge drafty hole in the wall that gave a clear view to the outside world. As he looked around, Gawain realized that this place wasn't all that different than the Pulford ruins that he had recently left behind. The ceiling was partially gone, and the winter's wind was able to enter through the many holes. On the plus side, the bed was soft and warm and Gawain was grateful for it. Nonetheless, he was determined to get out of there as quickly as possible and he tried to stand despite the stinging pain in his legs.

His flight was quickly halted by a loud boisterous voice.

"Excellent! You're awake. I was worried you'd miss your own feast!" exclaimed the man's voice that seemed unnaturally happy amongst the crumbling surroundings.

A tall, powerfully built man with short wavy brown hair and a smooth face entered with arms spread nearly as wide as his broad smile. Upon first glance, Gawain determined that this was what a knight was supposed to look like, and Gawain hoped that in his current condition he wouldn't have to fight this man. It didn't seem to be the case as the smiling lord plopped himself down upon the bed next to Gawain and clapped him on the shoulder. Gawain did his best to pretend that the slight tap on the shoulder didn't hurt like a clap of fire.

"Where am I?" croaked Gawain.

"Welcome to Hautdesert Castle!" said the man. "My humble home. I am your host, Sir Bertilak. At your service. Never mind the condition of the place. I've always preferred fresh air."

"How did I get here?" asked Gawain.

"Well, my most excellent friend, it seems you have a most excellent horse. He and my most excellent wife were able to bring you here," Sir Bertilak explained.

"Your wife?"

"I believe you're already acquainted with her."

Sir Bertilak gestured to the doorway. Gawain wrenched his head to see the blonde lady standing there in a new clean untorn dress. He let his head fall back to his pillow.

Wife? Gawain thought ruefully. *Why are the good ones always married?*

The blonde lady took a small hesitant step and it was just enough to clear the doorway so that she technically qualified as joining them in the room, although she seemed to be avoiding Gawain's attention.

"Lady Bertilak," said Gawain with a slight nod.

"I'm afraid in all the commotion I was quite rude and never got your name, good sir knight," said Lady Bertilak.

"Ah yes!" chimed in Sir Bertilak. "We must know the name of our guest of honor!"

"Gawain. Sir Gawain of the court of King Uther Pendragon," was the grizzled reply.

"Well, Sir Gawain of the court of King Uther Pendragon, tonight we honor you," declared Sir Bertilak in his loudest, most joyful tone. "You've brought my wife back safely, and I cannot give you enough thanks!"

Once again, Gawain struggled to sit up despite the pain that was screaming through his many wounds. Nonetheless, he did his best to hide it from his hosts. He certainly didn't want to show weakness before this fit handsome lord, and even less so in front of his crushingly beautiful lady.

"You don't understand. I have a duel I must get to," said Gawain between pained grimaces as he fought just to sit upright.

"I don't think you understand how bad of a condition you're in," remarked Sir Bertilak with an amused smirk as he watched Gawain's feeble attempts.

"I don't think The Green Knight will care about that," said Gawain.

Suddenly the light-hearted air vanished from the room as if it had been swept out by a quick breeze. Sir and Lady Bertilak exchanged a glance at the mere mention of the name, and Gawain could see the joy draining out of Sir Bertilak's face.

"Oh, him..."

"You know him? You know where I can find him?" asked Gawain with renewed intensity.

"I'm afraid we all do around these parts," said Sir Bertilak. "We try to stay away, of course, and sometimes it's easiest to avoid a trap when you know where it is."

"Then his chapel is in Old Swythamley?"

Sir Bertilak nodded with shudder, "Yes... Dreadful place. Not far from here. I can take you there myself, but first you must rest."

"No!" insisted Gawain.

"Yes," Sir Bertilak insisted right back, "Look, my good man, you're in a terrible state. You wouldn't be any good against him at the moment anyhow."

"Please, Sir Gawain, it would be my-" Lady Bertilak stopped herself suddenly with a quick bashful glance at her husband, "-our honor to have you here as our guest.

Gawain looked up at the lady. God, she was beautiful, especially when considered against the cold gray landscape that he had been living in for the past many moons. And her eyes were saying that she needed him. Or that's what Gawain wanted to believe they were saying anyway. Even if he was wrong about the lady, and he admitted that he probably was, Gawain grudgingly conceded to himself that it was a good idea to allow some time to rest and heal.

Finally, he grumbled and bowed his head in the closest thing he could muster to an acceptance of their offer.

Almost immediately, Sir Bertilak's jovial nature resurfaced as he said, "It's settled then! We'll get you patched up, and then you'll join us for the feast. Nelle, come in here!"

"No, I don't require any help," protested Gawain, but he quickly stopped as he spotted a tentative young woman appearing in the doorway with eyes cast downward.

"Nonsense, Nelle here will take excellent care of you. And we'll see you in the blink of an eye," said Sir Bertilak. "Now I must see that everything's taken care of. It's going to be quite a feast!"

With an athletic bound, Sir Bertilak rose from the bed and headed for the door. Gawain caught a brief pleased chuckle from the man as he ducked out of the room and was gone. Close on Sir Bertilak's heels was Lady Bertilak, but Gawain couldn't help but notice that she paused for a brief instant to cast him a longing backward glance. Once again, she had the effect of warming him all the way down to his fingertips and toes. And then, all too quickly, she was gone.

Now alone with the quiet young nurse, Gawain shifted uncomfortably as Nelle approached with a bowl of water and some rags. He had never been comfortable with people fussing over him, and her silent nature made it all the more awkward. Quietly she wrung the water out of a rag, and reached for Gawain's wounded arm. But he waved her away.

"You don't have to do that. It's just a few small insignificant scratches," said Gawain even as one of the bright red claw marks oozed slightly. "You can leave that here, and I'll take care of myself. Thank you for bringing it."

Nelle lowered her eyes further but didn't make any move to leave.

"I said you don't have to look after me," insisted Gawain.

"B-b-but, sir, they said I should see to your care," came her small shy voice.

"You don't have to call me 'sir!'" said Gawain as he bristled at the unwanted attention and willed the young woman to leave so that he could wallow alone in his own pain like any self-respecting knight.

"You-you don't have to yell," she said, and somehow her voice seemed to come out even smaller.

"I'm not yelling!" yelled Gawain. "I'm just saying-"

"I-I just thought that-" she stammered.

"I'm just saying I don't need to be fussed over!" Gawain shouted over her.

"I just thought you weren't supposed to be such a whimpering, monstrous baby…"

Gawain's jaw dropped in surprise. *Did she really just say what he thought she just said to him?!*

Sure enough, she had, and she wasn't finished yet as she continued, "I would've thought you were strong enough to handle a tiny little sting…"

In disbelief, Gawain stared at the tiny nurse. After a moment, she lifted her head just high enough to show sparkling mischievous eyes.

And a mousy wry smile.

Nelle was clearly pleased with herself, and as Gawain emitted a deep belly-laugh that somehow didn't cause him any pain, he admitted that he was pleased with her too. Now comfortable, Gawain extended his wounded arm to Nelle, and she began to dab carefully at it with her wet rag.

~ ~ ~

The sun had fallen, and the chill of the night had descended, but for the first time in weeks Gawain felt warm. Wrapped in clean bandages and dressed in soft comfortable clothes, Gawain emerged out into the cool night air to find a huge bonfire stretching upward and tickling the sky with its crackling fingers. Even from a distance of several dozen feet away, Gawain could feel the heat radiating from the raging fire, and its bright orange, red and yellow flames showered light all around the crowded fire pit. All around people had come to the fire's call and a celebration was underway. Gawain's heart lightened as he saw people eating and drinking and laughing and carousing. That was what Gawain had been longing for most and he felt a spring in his step as he worked his way into the crowd. Seemingly out of nowhere, someone thrust food and wine on him. Gawain accepted a hunk of charred meat, and bit into it with relish. Then he tipped back his goblet of wine and drank deeply of the sweet beverage feeling its warmth flooding down into his stomach. Gawain smacked his lips as a wide smile overtook his face for the first time in weeks.

"Thank the muses! Now there's a man who knows how to enjoy himself!"

Gawain turned to see a funny-looking man with fading red hair and streak of white along each temple. The man twisted a little beard as he strode toward Gawain with appraising eyes that bordered on twinkling madness.

"It feels better being the one to do the biting," replied Gawain apprehensively as he chewed his food and watched the thin man approach.

"Ah, yes! I heard all about your dance of death with the wolves. A thrilling tale...:" then the funny man cleared his throat and continued, "Let me see, let me see, let me see... Here we are... 'The mighty knight, Did lose a bite, In fearsome fight, Until the light, Did try to smite...' Um... Eh... It needs some work..."

At this point, Gawain was sure the man was mad.

"Oh! Dearest me to the gods!" cried the man as he smacked his forehead. "I should've explained to you my destiny amongst the many souls in this grand universe. You see, my name is Reynard. And I am a poet."

He declared it loudly and proudly and with a puff of his chest.

"Really?" was Gawain's wary response.

"Well, I dabble," admitted Reynard as his puffed chest deflated ever so slightly. "I have yet to do anything of great renown. I'm still searching for the right subject. Something funny yet exciting yet tragic yet uplifting yet... simple. That's not asking too much is it?"

The once confident poet now seemed to waffle as he toed at the ground and shrugged slightly. Apparently, he wasn't quite the wordsmith that he sought to be just yet, and he was still somewhat abashed by his own ambition.

But not to fear! Sir Gawain to the rescue!

The noble knight put his arm around Reynard's shoulder and pulled the poet in tight.

"I have the perfect subject for you. Listen to this... 'Sir Gawain and his Great Horse!'" said Gawain as he embraced the man who he was sure would make him famous. "You should probably be writing this down."

Reynard opened his mouth as he searched for the perfect response, but no words came. He was spared the need, however, as a hush fell over the party.

A single lovely note wafted through the air, and Gawain, Reynard, and all of the guests turned to see Lady Bertilak silhouetted in front of the blazing fire. She emitted her one perfect note for what seemed to be an impossibly long time until all eyes were on her and the note fell and died away. Then with the fire at her back, she began to sing:

"Oooh-Rah-De-Da-Sadie,
There was a Wind Lady,

She breezed where she pleased,

And she cooled all she met.

Through meadows and clover,

She knocked all things over,

She whistled and tickled,

Her chill did beset."

Gawain found himself grinning ear to ear as he watched the beautiful blonde lady begin to dance around the fire. Her simple ankle-length dress flicked and swished as she swayed along with the fire and cast dancing shadows upon the crowd. Every so often she would twist just right and her smooth pale face would be bathed in the pure golden light of the fire. It was beautiful and entrancing and Gawain imagined that she was looking right at him as she continued to sing:

"Aaah-Rah-Te-Ta-Eyre,

The King of the Fire,

He razed and he blazed,

And he scorched on and on.

Always consuming,

His tall pyres pluming,

So much did he touch,

And he smote til was gone."

Now her eyes definitely weren't leaving Gawain, and his gaze locked with hers as her wild beautiful dance crescendoed before the roaring fire. The flames crackled and rippled behind her as she swayed like the wind.

"Oooh-Aaah-Sadie-Eyre,

The wind met the fire,

They danced and they lanced

And made love all night long,

Her breeze urged him higher,

She raised on the fire,

They fed one another,

Then shrank like this song."

She finished with a flourish and a kick of her heels. Gawain had been the focus of enough adoring crowds to know when people liked what they saw, and it was clear that everyone had loved Lady Bertilak's performance as they cheered and whistled at her. Gracious and proper, she bowed to the crowd, crossed her ankles and curtseyed. But as she rose, Lady Bertilak lifted her eyes and locked her gaze on Gawain for a single shining moment. He stared right back, and despite the fact that he knew it was wrong, Gawain couldn't help but admit that he wanted her.

But as Lady Bertilak turned her head to nod and thank the rest of the clapping audience, Gawain caught a glance of someone who didn't seem to be enjoying herself.

The tiny nurse, Nelle, shook her head softly. Sadly. Full of melancholy.

Gawain frowned and tried to make sense of it. He was about to make his way over to the nurse when Sir Bertilak flanked him and threw his arm around Gawain. Once again, the tall handsome lord managed to clap his powerful hands on one of Gawain's fresh wounds. And once again, Gawain did all he could to hide the stabbing pain that ripped through his tender shoulder.

"Quite the celebration, eh, my friend?" said Sir Bertilak with a slight hiccup.

"Yes it is," agreed Gawain.

"We're a simple people, but we do enjoy ourselves," said Sir Bertilak with a wide smile and a slightly less sturdy voice than Gawain had previously heard from the man.

Sir Bertilak tipped his mug back, and Gawain felt obliged to do the same. The two men took a long drink and when they were finished Gawain couldn't remember ever having been in less pain. As Sir Bertilak slipped out a slight belch, Gawain took in the state of affairs of the place.

"Maybe you've enjoyed yourself a bit too much," said Gawain inclining his head toward the crumbling castle. "You might want to spend a bit of time on castle upkeep."

"Ah, but that's the true beauty of the feast," shot back Sir Bertilak, "Despite our troubles, some good food, some good wine, and some good song help to lift everyone's spirits. How could anyone worry when they have a celebration like this to look forward to every night?"

"I like a fine meal washed down with a delicious drink as much as the next man, this is truly spectacular, by the way," said Gawain as he bit off another bite, "But the you can't blind yourself to reality. Tell me, what has befallen this place?"

Before Gawain could press it any further, Sir Bertilak cut across him, "Nothing to worry yourself over, my friend. I promise you, I have it well under control."

"Please, I might be able to help."

Sir Bertilak waved a dismissive hand.

"The lands are running wild. We've had some trouble with our crops. And with our waters. And the surrounding beasts have turned against us," said Sir Bertilak with as much indifference as he might if he were discussing a slight cold.

Gawain stared at him in disbelief. He had been in some truly dire situations, but this wasn't something to just dismiss. This was almost as bad as the time that Gawain had battled a sphinx to free a village from plague.

"I promise you, it's nothing to be afraid of, Sir Gawain," said Sir Bertilak. "Come the spring, all will be right again."

"Once I've finish my journey, and have fulfilled my vow with the Green Knight. You have my word that I'll come back to help you," swore Gawain with a hand over his heart.

"You truly are an unimpeachable hero, aren't you?" said Bertilak with a laugh.

"I wouldn't say that..."

And Gawain's eyes once again fell upon the lovely form of Lady Bertilak who was still beautifully illuminated by the raging fire.

"I simply owe you for your kindness," said Gawain as he quickly turned his attention back to Sir Bertilak.

"Ha! You owe me?! I owe you, Sir Gawain! I owe you everything," cried the happy lord.

"We can just call things even then," said Gawain and he offered his hand to Sir Bertilak.

But Sir Bertilak looked past the hand as something else occurred to him, "Even...? Hmmm? I'll tell you what? Tomorrow I'll be out on the hunt, nothing to worry about, it's simply to keep an eye out for any beasts that might be becoming too bold and might pose a threat. But I want you to do something for me while I'm away."

Gawain froze. His eyes darted to Lady Bertilak once more as he wondered if he was really going to be given permission to follow his heart's desire.

"I'll make you a deal," began Sir Bertilak, "Whatever I catch on the hunt, I'll give to you. And whatever you may receive in the castle, you can give to me."

"I doubt I'll catch anything tomorrow," was Gawain's honest reply.

"It's a castle with no walls," laughed Sir Bertilak. "I imagine a man of your stature can at least manage to catch a mouse or two!"

"Fair enough. We have a gentleman's agreement."

And, once again, Gawain extended his hand. This time Sir Bertilak seemed only too happy to shake it. Then to seal the deal even further, the two men clinked their mugs together and, once more, drank deeply of the sweet spirits inside. This time, neither of them resurfaced until their mugs were completely empty.

They laughed and smiled and, all around them, the celebration raged on.

~ ~ ~

CHAPTER 12

Harts and Hearts

As the morning's sunlight crept in through the gaping hole in Gawain's bedroom wall, the formidable knight found himself pinned down by an entirely different kind of foe. His own pounding head. Under other circumstances, Gawain might've been alarmed or even annoyed by the mostly non-existent wall of his bedroom, but at the moment, he was grateful for the cool wind that blew in and caressed his slightly sweaty forehead. Gawain lay spread out in his bed, clutched his head, and covered his eyes.

"Damn, that sun!" he moaned. "Ugh... The only thing I expect to have to show for today is a vicious, throbbing, pounding, bloody head..."

A delicate giggling from the doorway made Gawain realize he was no longer alone. He uncovered his eyes ever so slightly and the morning sun stabbed at his bloodshot eyes, but he saw Nelle standing there with arms full of bandages.

"Go away..." he groaned.

"I'm, I'm just here to..." she said in her soft tentative voice before clearing her throat and declaring politely, "My lord, I'm here to change your bandages."

"Be quick with it then..." came his less polite reply.

Nelle approached, and quietly stripped away the older dirty bandages. As she pulled them away and began to clean Gawain's wounds, he realized with some surprise that much of his pain was already gone. He caught a glimpse of his own bare flesh and saw that it was healing quite quickly. Nelle applied new clean bandages to Gawain's injured skin, and once she had it fully wrapped, she closed her eyes and traced a strange circular symbol over the covered wound. Gawain cast her a questioning yet fascinated look.

"It's a binding symbol," she said so quietly that he could barely understand her. "It may be silly, but-"

"Not silly at all!" roared Gawain and then winced at his own loud voice.

Nonetheless, Gawain sat up and twisted around to grab the breastplate of his armor out of a pile in the corner. He proudly lifted it and showed it off to Nelle as he traced his finger along a chipped painted rune.

"This is from a Celtic clan I met on an adventure. It's for protection. "

Nelle smiled, and Gawain thought that it was as close as he'd ever seen the nurse get to beaming. It was lovely. After a pause, Nelle took a deep breath and drew another more complicated symbol over a bandage on Gawain's leg.

"My family's been using that one for centuries. It's meant to quicken the blood clots," Nelle said.

"Your family? You come from a long line of healers then?" asked Gawain.

"Something like that…" she replied and her eyes looked away to examine what she must have considered an impressive crack in the wall instead of into Gawain's eyes.

But Gawain didn't seem to mind as he waved his newly wrapped limbs.

"Well, I feel better already," he declared. "I would hazard a guess that your family would be truly proud. You seem to have quite the gift, my fine nurse."

From that moment onward, a soft smile was a permanent fixture upon Nelle's small round face. Quietly, she continued dressing his wounds, pausing from time to time to place her hands on an injury while she muttered a strange prayer under her breath, or she would trace another of her complicated interlocking healing symbols along one of Gawain's wounds. Gawain never failed to feel a slight flush of goose flesh with each of the silent woman's strange techniques. He had seen enough bizarre and wondrous acts in the world to know that the vast majority of these kinds of shows were simply superstition and wishes. Nonetheless, he also knew that they seldom hurt if they were well-intentioned. He lay silently and did his best to absorb whatever good energies she might be bestowing upon him, even though he doubted there was much actual magic behind it.

"If you're interested, my lord…" Nelle said after nearly an hour of her healing techniques. "I do have another treatment. It might help your 'vicious, throbbing, pounding, bloody head.'"

"Eh? What's that?" asked Gawain eagerly.

"More wine?"

That mousy wry smile of hers was back.

Gawain laughed and shook his head in mock disgust.

~ ~ ~

Unimpeded by leaves, the bright sun shone through the barren trees as Sir Bertilak, his men and their horses slowly patrolled the deserted forest in search of possible dangers. The breath of each of the men came out in thick clear bursts of mist, but they all stayed strong against the cold. The hooves of the horses beat clearly upon the hard frozen ground, and Sir Bertilak took the lead as he strained his ears for any sign of trouble. At his side, however, Reynard was making it difficult to concentrate.

"'His name was Gawain, He tussled with pain,' No... No... That won't do...," muttered Reynard as he absent-mindedly try to compose a poem. "'The Tale of Gawain, Both Bold and Profane,' No, that doesn't sound quite right either."

"Reynard..." interjected Sir Bertilak.

But Reynard pressed forward, "The problem with Gawain is the only words that rhyme with his name are so bleak. 'Pain,' 'Rain,' 'Slain.'"

"Reynard, could we please have some silence?" asked Sir Bertilak trying his best to maintain his generally jovial attitude.

"You're just jealous because I'm not working on a poem for you," laughed Reynard. "Worry not, my lord, my muse is never far from you."

"It's not that, my friend, I have full faith in your poetic prowess," said Sir Bertilak as he reached over to Reynard's horse and patted his friend on the leg. "It's just that we're on the hunt at the moment. This is rather serious business, what with the safety of the lands at stake, and I need to concentrate."

"We haven't seen so much as a lark all morning," opined Reynard.

"I would welcome a lark," said Bertilak. "I've been following these faint tracks…"

Sir Bertilak pointed at faint hoof prints scratched into the dirt. An ordinary man wouldn't have noticed them at all, but Sir Bertilak wasn't an ordinary man.

"Ah! Hooves! Well spotted, my excellent lord," said Reynard, clearly delighted at Sir Bertilak's skill on the hunt. "Another horse, you think?"

"Too narrow to be a horse."

With his eyes locked on the tracks, Sir Bertilak followed them diligently. After several yards, he was rewarded as they became better defined and more numerous. Of course, this created new concerns.

"And I think there's more than one," noted Sir Bertilak with just the faintest hint of alarm.

As a rule, Sir Bertilak never allowed himself to be alarmed. He had always tried to face the world and his duties with an implacable sense of optimism, and it had always suited him. When something bad or challenging presented itself to him, he simply didn't worry about it. Instead he would act. He had always found that doing something, anything really, was better than fretting and stressing. Overall, it had worked for him quite well.

His father had died when Sir Bertilak was still only fourteen years of age.

Not a problem. Just act.

The people in Hautdesert Castle and the surrounding lands were looking to him now.

Don't worry about it. Just act.

Food, wine and resources were running low and people were worried.

Nothing to be concerned about. Just feast and be merry and act.

Sir Bertilak would be the first to admit that the current state of his castle and the surrounding lands was less than ideal, but he pressed on anyway. He refused to worry. Instead, he got up every morning and went out in search of food to eat and enemies to vanquish. He had lost several men in the process, it was true, but he still had a stolid loyal crew to work with. And for the time being, they still had some wine for that evening's feast. And there was more than enough dried wood all around to start a fire. Life could be worse.

They continued to follow the tracks as they became more and more numerous. Sir Bertilak came upon a patch of earth that was almost entirely scratched and scored with the tracks. There were so many that even Reynard would've be hard pressed to miss them.

"My lord...?" whispered the poet.

But Sir Bertilak waved him away as he became engrossed with the dozens, if not hundreds, of marks that littered the ground.

"It's all right, Reynard," said Sir Bertilak, not bothering to glance upward. "Although I would say we've stumbled upon the makings of a feast tonight."

"My lord…" stammered Reynard again, "…look…"

Sir Bertilak finally raised his head and saw what was causing the normally easy-going Reynard's shaky voice. It was hard to miss. A short distance ahead, perched upon a high ledge, was a small army of tall powerful harts. But these weren't like any deer that Sir Bertilak had ever seen before. Their mighty antlers had sharp points and razor edges. Their mouths foamed around bared fangs.

And their eyes were all glowing emerald green.

Sir Bertilak's light-hearted mood disappeared. He kept his eyes locked on the strange beasts as his hand fell to the sword at his side.

"Weapons, men…"

~ ~ ~

Back in his cramped crumbling bedroom, Gawain sat on his bed with his legs crossed. He faced Nelle who sat beside him and laughed as she traced another looping symbol along Gawain's broad ribs. As she did so, Gawain burst out laughing.

"Ah! That tickles!"

"It's the trifold arrow! It's supposed to tickle!" scolded Nelle as she playfully slapped Gawain on the shoulder.

"And what's this one for?" asked Gawain.

"To make your piss like a raging river!" she declared.

The two of them roared with laughter once more, and it made
Gawain feel better than any silly charm or spell she might've been
casting upon him possibly could have. He had to admit that this
particular nurse had some excellent powers for improving his
mood. She reached out to draw another symbol upon a bandage
around his calf, when a voice made them both pause.

"Nelle. That'll be all."

Both Gawain and Nelle stopped laughing and turned quickly to
the door. Lady Bertilak stood framed in the doorway as she looked
in at Gawain. It was clear that she was really taking him in. And,
very quickly, Gawain was really taking her in too.

Nelle's face dropped and her voice, which was playful and
bright a few moments ago, steadied to become proper and low, "I'm
sorry, m'lady. I was only.."

"It's quite all right," said Lady Bertilak.

"She and I were just sharing spells," Gawain said, leaping to
Nelle's defense.

But Lady Bertilak pleasantly waved it all away with a bright
smile, "Oh, not to worry. I'm honestly not upset in the least. But,
Nelle dear, would you mind leaving us so that I might have a
moment to speak with Sir Gawain privately?"

"But I was just finishing-"

"Leave us," said Lady Bertilak just a bit more firmly this time.

It was enough. Nelle bowed to Gawain, and then she quickly
hurried past Lady Bertilak and disappeared out the door. Gawain

heard her quick scurrying footsteps as the nurse rushed down the hall and was gone.

"She was only showing me some of her healing symbols. Don't be angry with her," said Gawain.

"Oh, I could never be angry with Nelle. In many ways, I don't know who serves who. She's a sweet, gentle thing…," and here Lady Bertilak forcefully pulled the door shut behind her.

"Unlike me."

Gawain gazed at Lady Bertilak. And she returned to him a soft faint smile that melted his heart. It was a while before either of them felt the need to speak.

"I… don't know if you should be in here, Lady Bertilak," said Gawain trying to hide the husky tenor that his voice had just taken on.

"I don't know if I should be either," said Lady Bertilak.

She sat down on the bed beside Gawain anyway.

"But I had to see how you were doing. You were so brave yesterday, riding to my rescue, my own knight in slightly painted armor."

Gawain smiled at her, and she looked as if she was battling with herself, trying to force herself to do something that she wasn't entirely sure was a good idea.

"I can't stop thinking about you," she admitted in a soft demure voice that was both alluring and terrified. "And my husband is busy elsewhere at the moment."

~ ~ ~

Sir Bertilak certainly was elsewhere. And he certainly was busy. He was locked into an epic battle with the unnatural other-worldly army of green-eyed harts. And he was having the time of his life. It was dangerous. It was cursed. It was perhaps a battle that could be the end of Sir Bertilak and all he held dear.

But he had never been one to worry.

Sir Bertilak howled a war cry to urge on Reynard and his other half-dozen men. Each of them was rising boldly to the challenge, and Sir Bertilak was proud of each and every one of them. Sure, none of them seemed to be enjoying themselves quite as much as Sir Bertilak. In fact, several of them looked like they might be sick at any moment. Sir Bertilak was proud of them, nonetheless.

The brave lord brought his sword down with a mighty clash upon the head of a hart, but his blade failed to cut through the jagged antlers. Instead they resounded with a rattle like steel upon steel. Again and again, Sir Bertilak slashed at the antlers and, again and again, it did no good.

"I'm not sure blows to the head are going to work, my lord!" shouted Reynard as he too had no luck with his sword.

In the blink of an eye, Sir Bertilak cast his sword aside and drew the bow that he had tucked into a holster on his saddle. On his back, was a quiver full of arrows, and with the speed and confidence of an expert bowmen, he drew an arrow into place.

"Well, there's only one way to take down a hart!"

Twang! He let his arrow fly, and it buried itself deep into the breast of one of the harts. That did the trick. The beast went down.

In a flash, Sir Bertilak had a new arrow drawn and placed in his bow. He fired again, and another four-legged terror was dead. Another arrow. Another heart of a hart. And another. And another.

The charging harts fell all around, and several of the men were finally able to breathe easy once more.

"How's this as a poem for you, Reynard!?" cried Sir Bertilak.

The poet was only too happy to heap his effusive praise as he called back, "An epic, my lord! Truly an epic!"

~   ~   ~

"I want to thank you for saving my life, Sir Gawain," said Lady Bertilak as she slid just a bit closer to Gawain on his bed.

"Not necessary, m'lady," said Gawain humbly, but he was enjoying their closer proximity. "I'm a knight. Saving beautiful ladies is all part of the job."

"You think I'm beautiful then?"

She leaned in to kiss him. Her lips looked soft and red and inviting. But, and it pained him more than a thousand wolf bites, Gawain stopped her, and gently held her at arm's length.

"As much as I'd like to, and believe me I would like to, I can't," said Gawain. "I didn't save you for this."

Lady Bertilak slid on the bed once more, but this time in the opposite direction.

"God... I knew you were a brave man," she sighed and sounded both disappointed and somewhat relieved. "I didn't know you were a good one too."

"And your husband seems to be one, as well," said Gawain.

"He is. He's kind and courageous and true-"

But Lady Bertilak's voice trailed off as her face lost its color and became ashen. She seemed at a loss for words, but then forced herself to continue.

"-But I'm not sure he can save us."

"What do you mean?" asked Gawain.

"My husband wouldn't like me to tell you," said the lady, "But I suspect you already know…"

"That the Green Knight has a grip on these lands too," said Gawain venturing a guess and finishing her thought.

Lady Bertilak nodded.

"You mustn't think any less of us," said Lady Bertilak quickly. "Sir Bertilak ignored many entreaties and taunts for a long, long time. He's a humble man."

"That's one thing we don't have in common then…" said Gawain somewhat as a means to console her and somewhat to console himself.

"The Green Knight has many tricks. He takes many guises," warned Lady Bertilak ominously. "When he sets his sight upon someone, he'll do whatever it takes to defeat them. Despite being so close, Sir Bertilak had always been able to stand firm against him. It enraged the Green Knight. Then one day, he learned of my husband's skill with a bow. The Green Knight finally succeeded in fooling my husband into an archery contest. Sir Bertilak struck the Green Knight with a perfect shot into the heart. And the Green Knight casually drew it out and tossed it aside."

"Then he demanded the right to return the shot in a year and a day," said Gawain feeling that familiar pit in his stomach.

Lady Bertilak nodded again.

"But Sir Bertilak didn't go?" asked Gawain in some surprise. Sir Bertilak had struck Gawain as an uncommonly brave man and one who seemed like he would've accepted his destiny and walked bravely into the flames.

"How could he?" cried Lady Bertilak. "It would've meant certain death. No one can survive against the Green Knight."

Gawain sighed and now his face became grave. Everywhere that he went there was evidence of the Green Knight's invincibility. There hadn't been any sign that Gawain had any hope of success.

"Ever since that day, our lands have turned against us," said Lady Bertilak. "The waters went dirty. The soil refused to let anything grow. And all manner of animal have become furious and terrible. And the Green Knight promised to come back, and finish the job."

"Not if I can help it," stated Gawain.

"There's no way you can defeat him," said Lady Bertilak shaking her head sadly.

"Maybe I don't need to defeat him. Maybe I can simply take him with me," said Gawain. "And free your lands in the process."

"I don't think I've ever met anyone like you, Sir Gawain. The world will be worse off without you in it," said Lady Bertilak as her voice dropped.

In that moment, Lady Bertilak leaned in without warning and kissed Gawain on the cheek. He snapped out of his trance, and looked at her as his cheek burned warmly where her lips had touched him.

"For luck."

Then she rose, crossed the room, opened the door and was gone. Gawain looked to the doorway and still felt her presence even as she disappeared. Something about her reached down into his fingertips and toes. His heart swelled for her. Suddenly, he found himself on his feet, and he was about to follow after her when a bellowing call snapped him out of it.

"Gawain! Ho!"

Sir Gawain looked around in confusion until he realized that the voice had come from outside. He walked over to the gaping hole in his wall and looked out to see a band of men approaching from the distance. Sir Bertilak led Reynard and the other six men who looked like warriors returning from battle. They were dirty and bloodied and beaming with pride.

"I've got a good harvest for you!" called Sir Bertilak with his broad smile stretched across his handsome face.

The beaming lord gestured to several wagons that their horses dragged behind. They were piled high with the dead carcasses of once-mighty harts.

Sir Bertilak grinned as he shouted, "Get down here, my friend! Tonight's going to be a feast to remember!"

~ ~ ~

CHAPTER 13

The Second Feast

The last rays of sunshine were dying away as Gawain met Sir Bertilak on the south side of the castle where the massive fire pit was once again being prepared for the upcoming feasts. Sir Bertilak joyfully shouted orders at the servants who seemed happy to carry them out. Several men piled up logs into the fire circle, but it clearly wasn't enough as Sir Bertilak urged them on.

"More wood! I want the stack as tall as a man. As tall as my good friend, Sir Gawain, that is!" the handsome lord laughed. "I want it even bigger and brighter and grander than last night! A fire that will be seen for miles around!"

Then Sir Bertilak pointed at several more servants who were unloading the wagons full of dead harts.

"Take the beasts upwind to carve them. Save us the stench. But we'll have fine steaks tonight!"

All of the servants dutifully did as they were told, and they dragged the wagons away, and brought in more and more armfuls of firewood. Gawain watched it all with a degree of apprehension.

"Should we really be eating them?" asked Gawain trying to hide his look of disgust and failing badly.

"Why not?!" cried Sir Bertilak clearly not noticing Gawain's grimace. "It's what we've been eating for months. It's what you ate last night."

Gawain dry-heaved this time, and Sir Bertilak couldn't help but see it.

"Don't worry about it, my friend. I insist you eat it. It's all my gift to you, after all," said Sir Bertilak as he threw an arm around Gawain.

"Should we really be celebrating tonight?" asked Gawain with his eyes on the pile of carcasses and remembering the wolves that he had faced the day before. "How can you be sure that we won't be ambushed?"

But Sir Bertilak shook his head and said, "We've never once had a problem at night. These beasts give us our peace, it's only during the day that we have anything to worry about."

This seemed strange to Gawain. Generally, dark forces preferred to operate in, well, the dark. He opened his mouth to argue, but Sir Bertilak quickly cut him off.

"I tell you there is nothing to worry about. Nothing to fret or stress or concern yourself with!" said Sir Bertilak, before adding with a sly grin. "However, you and I had an agreement, and I'm starting to think you're trying to get out of your side of it. Now tell me, my friend, have you got anything for me?"

Gawain paused uncomfortably. All he could think of was the kiss that Lady Bertilak had given him mere moments ago. His cheek still flushed so strongly that he was sure Sir Bertilak must be able to notice it. Gawain convinced himself he was being foolish, however, and so he cast his mind about for something that he could offer the jovial lord.

"Just some new bandages, my lord, if you'd like to share them…" Gawain offered and he started to pull at the tightly wrapped strips of cloth.

But Sir Bertilak stopped him with a laugh, "No, no, no! You need those much more than I, my friend! Although I must say, you are looking better already."

"I've always been a fast healer," boasted Gawain, and then feeling he should show at least a little modesty, he added, "And your wife's nurse is excellent."

"Nelle certainly is," said Sir Bertilak. "But, Sir Gawain, you're avoiding our game! Are you sure you've nothing else to show from your day?"

"It's been a quiet day."

"Nothing at all?! Surely, you're holding out on me," said Sir Bertilak and he noticed that Gawain wasn't making eye contact. "Come now, Sir Gawain, that wasn't the agreement!"

A funny smirk crossed Gawain's face. Then he quickly leaned in and kissed Sir Bertilak on the cheek. Sir Bertilak was a big talker but this quieted him for a moment. His jaw dropped as he stared at Gawain in confusion. Then comprehension dawned on him and he burst out in delighted laughter.

"You dog! Who?!"

"Ah, but that wasn't part of the game," shrugged Gawain.

Sir Bertilak continued to laugh heartily as he slapped an arm around Gawain. Then he turned to declare to the night and anyone who was near enough to hear,

"Let us get this feast started! We have a lot to celebrate!"

Almost on the word, a spark was struck, and the pile of wood burst into flames.

~ ~ ~

The new bonfire raged tall and hot. The celebration was well underway. Every man, woman, and child had poured out of the castle and in from the nearby surrounding lands to crowd around the fire. They laughed and smiled. They ate dripping delicious food. They drank tall mugs of plentiful wine.

And joy was shared by all.

Sir Bertilak worked the crowd, bouncing from group to group as he charmed anyone who might seem like they were having less than the time of their lives. Lady Bertilak followed dutifully behind her husband, but she had never felt the easy skill to converse that Sir Bertilak so excelled at. Gawain glimpsed the beautiful lady from across the fire, and he couldn't help but note that she seemed somewhat subdued and ill at ease.

For his part, Gawain had found himself surrounded by several of the men that had been out on the day's hunt including Reynard who was doing his best to enthusiastically recap the day.

"There must've been a thousand of them! Am I right?" declared Reynard.

Several of the other men just laughed and shook their heads. Gawain only half listened as he continued trying to catch a glimpse of Lady Bertilak.

"An army! A horde! A monsoon of beasts!" continued Reynard impressively. "Pouring down upon us with all the intensity of a storm of brimstone!"

Gawain looked across the fire once more and his eyes fell upon a small group of servants who didn't seem to be enjoying themselves quite as much as the others. At the center of the group was Nelle. Even from this distance, Gawain could tell that the small nurse hadn't been talking as she picked tentatively at a steak that looked to be larger than her head. It seemed clear that she wasn't taken in by the celebration all around her.

"Excuse me, my good men," said Gawain as he extricated himself from the group of men who barely seemed to notice as Reynard continued his embellishments.

"Their hooves rattles like thunder! Like an earthquake!"

Gawain moved away and crossed through throngs of happy people. More than once he bumped or cajoled a stranger, but as he tried to apologize he was met with glad smiles and hearty handshakes. Nearly everyone seemed to be having a wonderful time. Nearly everyone but Nelle.

"You don't seem to be enjoying yourself," whispered Gawain as he sidled up beside her.

"Of course I am. Look, see... I have monster meat," she said.

"Ugh... I disposed of mine as quickly as possible," Gawain said with a shudder. "The fire hides all."

"A wonderful idea," Nelle said. Then she glanced around to make sure no one was watching her, "Keep a lookout for me."

Gawain stepped in front of Nelle to shield her as she deftly crept up to the fire, faked a cough, and tossed her steak into the flames.

"Well done," complimented Gawain.

"The meat? Or the maneuver?" asked Nelle with her wry mousy smile.

Gawain laughed, but he still couldn't help but observe, "You still don't seem very relieved. What's the real problem?"

"Nothing... There's nothing wrong," she said with her eyes cast downward once again.

"You can tell me. I know what's going on around here. Lady Bertilak told me all about-"

But Nelle cut him off as she said in a low angry voice unlike anything Gawain had ever heard her use before, "No one has a clue what they're really facing here."

Gawain stared at Nelle, dumbfounded by her sudden gloominess.

"They feast and they make merry. All because they killed a few deer," she continued. "But worse will come. And they'll keep coming. And coming. Until the job is done."

"Sir Bertilak seems up to the task of holding off the vicious beasts," argued Gawain.

"For now. But he can't stop it."

"Why don't the people just leave then?"

"They're simple people," shrugged Nelle. "And they're afraid. And being lied to. Sir Bertilak keeps them happy with wine and feasts. He convinces them that everything is all right and they have nothing to worry about. But he's leading them to their doom."

She finally seemed to remember that Gawain had befriended Sir Bertilak, and she fell silent. She dropped her eyes again in her proper deferential way. For the first time, Gawain recognized the sadness that was there.

"I'm sorry, Sir Gawain," she muttered. "I shouldn't have-"

"I'm going to save you all, Nelle," promised Gawain. "I'm going to stop this."

"You'll try. You'll fail."

Her head was still bowed. And Gawain tried to get her to look at him, but she stubbornly refused as she kept her eyes locked on the ground. Gently, he touched her chin and raised her head. He looked into her eyes and saw for the first time that they were different colors. One was a dark stormy blue. The other a pale green. He wasn't sure why, but her eyes gave Gawain pause. There was something strange about them.

A sudden cheer from the crowd snatched Gawain's attention, and he turned to see what had prompted the outburst of applause. Very quickly, he spotted Reynard prancing in front of the fire with all eyes on him as he sang,

"*Through darkest night,*

Through fiercest fight,

The fearsome beasts

Quaked at our sight!

We fell upon

The vicious throng

Our mighty reach

Was swift and strong!"

Gawain laughed as he watched the funny thin man flailing and gesticulating wildly as he reenacted the thrilling battle. With a broad smile, Gawain turned to see if the song was having the same calming effect on Nelle. But she was gone.

"Their antlers slashed,

Their fierce hooves crashed,

And foaming mouths

Spit, bit, and gnashed.

Our arrows clashed,

Our hammers smashed,

The things fell low

As strong we lashed!"

Ignoring the silly song, Gawain scanned the crowd, but the small shy nurse was nowhere to be found.

"The beasts fell back,

From our attack,

Our might hack,

Left them no slack.

Saved by the sword,

Of our Mighty Lord,

The brave and righteous

Bertilak!"

Everyone cheered as Reynard finished the song with a high note that he couldn't have possibly hoped to hit. The mangled finale made the whole thing more entertaining, however, and as Reynard bowed to the crowd, everyone raised their mugs and echoed the final lines of the song.

"The brave and righteous Bertilak!"

For his part, Sir Bertilak magnanimously waved away the effusive praise despite the fact that he was clearly loving every minute of it.

"This is a celebration for all of us, isn't it?!" declared Sir Bertilak, his generous nature on full display. "More wine! More music! More dancing!"

The tireless musicians were only too happy to oblige as they picked at their strings and pounded upon their drums and the fire circle was once again filled with a lively tune. Aided on by full bellies of food and wine, the many people partnered up and began to dance. The crowd swirled and swayed with the music, but Gawain continued to seek Nelle. Her ominous words stuck in his mind and he wanted to find out what else she might know. Not without a certain amount of difficulty, Gawain ducked and dodged around the twirling dancers as he called,

"Nelle? Have you seen Nelle? The little nurse? Have you seen her?"

Suddenly, a soft tender hand grabbed his shoulder. He spun to see Lady Bertilak looking as beautiful as ever in the flickering firelight. She took his hand and threw her other arm around his waist.

"Dance with me," said the lovely blonde lady.

"Have you seen Nelle?" asked Gawain.

Gawain could've been imagining it, but it seemed like the mere mention of Nelle's name made Lady Bertilak shudder slightly.

"Forget about her for the moment," said Lady Bertilak with soft insistence. "Just dance with me."

Gawain opened his mouth to protest, but Lady Bertilak pressed a finger to his lips.

"Shhh... Just for tonight. Just for this moment. Please. You make me feel safe in a way that I haven't for many moons..."

Her gentle whisper brought Gawain back and he finally looked into her eyes. Big and longing and sparkling with the crackling flames. How could he resist? They danced. Slowly at first as they melted into the crowd. Then faster and faster. Gawain's skills with the sword were nearly unrivalled and it just wasn't possible to get that good without having a knack for footwork. As he spun and twirled Lady Bertilak he was determined to show her every bit of his prodigious skill on the dance floor. And he could tell that the beautiful lady was thrilled by the display. They laughed and smiled and managed to look exquisitely happy.

Off to the side, however, Sir Bertilak watched Gawain's display with his wife.

And he didn't look happy at all.

~ ~ ~

CHAPTER 14
On the Hunt

As the morning sun peaked in through the hole in his wall, Gawain stirred in his bed. The cool breeze made him stiff, but he had none of the aches and pains that the previous night's festivities had brought on. He twisted in bed, and was pleasantly surprised to notice that he felt little to no pain in his many wounds. Despite having nearly been a meal for wolves just two days prior, he was now almost entirely healed. Gawain sat up to marvel at this, but then reminded himself that he'd always been a quick healer and there was no reason to believe that this time should be any different. He stretched his back and cracked his joints and felt his old familiar swagger beginning to creep back in. He was nearly back to his old self. He had a full belly of food and wine from the past two days' feasts and the renewing effect of that couldn't be understated. A warm beam of sunshine fell across his face and for one fleeting moment, he felt like the legendary knight, Sir Gawain, again.

It didn't last.

Almost as soon as the relief had washed over him, it receded quickly like the waves upon the beach. A pang hit his stomach as he remembered that his recovery only made it that much more certain that he would soon have to continue his journey to the chapel in Old Swythamley and seek the Green Knight. Unfortunately, the more time Gawain had spent in Hautdesert Castle, as pleasant as it had been, the more he had seen signs of hopelessness that facing the Green Knight brought. It seemed that Sir Bertilak was doing an admirable job of keeping his people's morale up amidst the darkening circumstances, but that was seeming to balance more and more on a knife's edge and was certain to stumble soon. Gawain had seen the looks of terror and misery on the faces of Lady Bertilak and Nelle when the Green Knight's name was simply raised. There had to be whispers amongst all of the servants, and the surrounding commoners that relied on Sir Bertilak and his castle must be feeling the strain too.

Once more, Gawain made a vow to himself that he would see his promise through to the end. He couldn't risk subjecting his own home to the unnatural desolation that was now sweeping across Hautdesert Castle. Nonetheless, he felt an icy chill when he contemplated what it would take on his part to stop the terrible grip of the Green Knight from seizing upon Uther Pendragon, Arthur and Tintagel.

And Gawain hoped that he might be able to find a way to help Sir Bertilak and his people, as well.

Almost as if in answer, Sir Bertilak came striding down the hallway and passed by Gawain's bedroom door. Gawain caught a glimpse of the tall handsome lord pulling on his riding gloves, and Gawain figured that it was nearly time for the day's hunt to depart.

Leaping out of his bed, the mighty knight called to Sir Bertilak, "My lord! Leaving so soon? The sun has barely risen."

"Ah, Sir Gawain, I trust you slept well," said Sir Bertilak with a perfunctory nod, and Gawain noticed that the tone was much more cold and formal than usual.

"Your feast last night helped. And I'm healing surprisingly fast," said Gawain.

"Glad to hear it," said Sir Bertilak, once again with a strange bristle to his voice. "I'm sorry I can't see to your breakfast. I'm off for the day's hunt."

"I see that. So does our previous arrangement still stand?"

Finally, the merest hint of a smile broke across Sir Bertilak's face. His frosty demeanor quickly melted away as he turned to Gawain and spread out his arms in one of his signature friendly gestures.

"It does! Of course, it does, my friend! I'm glad to see that you have embraced my little game, my good friend. Once again, my good dear friend, at tonight's feast we will share whatever treasures the day may bring us. Whatever I catch is yours."

"And I'll try to slay some spiders here for you," said Gawain.

"Ah, I still think you held out on me yesterday. I'm going to be more strict tonight," said Sir Bertilak and then he turned to shout, "Nelle!"

Seemingly out of nowhere, the tiny nurse appeared from around the corner with her head properly bowed. Just the sight of her relaxed Gawain a bit. He had been worried that their strange encounter the night before might have soured her on him. That would've been quite a shame since, over the past couple of days, he had really grown fond of his nurse, her fascinating healing techniques, and her soft tickling hands.

"Get him cleaned up," ordered Sir Bertilak. "He's starting to stink."

And with a playful wink, Sir Bertilak quickly strode away and was gone. Nelle shuffled quietly into Gawain's room and began to set out her assortment of bandages. As she did so, she quickly darted her head toward Gawain and stole a sniff of his armpit. She grimaced with just a bit too much enthusiasm to be entirely truthful as she moaned.

"Does he expect me to work miracles?"

Gawain couldn't help but laugh.

~ ~ ~

Once again, Sir Bertilak, Reynard, and his men journeyed out into the cold barren forest. Once again, their horse's hooves resounded on the hard frozen ground. And once again, Reynard couldn't manage to be quiet.

"After last night's rousing success, I need an equally thrilling follow-up..." mused Reynard in his musical lilting tone that couldn't help but relax the other men. "What do you think? Should I try my hand at one of the ancient legends? Odysseus? Or Aeneus? Perhaps I could bring new life to the love story of Cleopatra? Or should I stay closer to home and dive into the adventures of the great Sir Gawain tonight?"

"Can we not talk about our distinguished guest at the moment?" asked Sir Bertilak as he reflexively twitched at the mere mention of the name, as if it was an annoying fly that kept landing on his head despite his best efforts to wave it away.

Reynard wasn't about to let it lie, however, as he prodded, "Oooh... Is someone getting hero envy?"

"It's not that at all," said Sir Bertilak stubbornly.

"I assure you, my lord, Sir Gawain is merely a candle that helps to illuminate your splendor," said Reynard.

"I have nothing but respect for him," mumbled Sir Bertilak.

"He is little more than a preface to the great epic that is you," continued Reynard.

"I am not trying to compare us," said Sir Bertilak through gritted teeth.

"Gawain isn't fit to-"

"I can't hear the trees with your constant prattle!"

Sir Bertilak's sudden outburst caused Reynard to fall silent for a long moment. The normally loquacious poet tied his tongue and managed to look only slightly abashed at the dressing down. For his part, Sir Bertilak forced himself to scan the forest and pointedly avoided the gaze of his friend. Several long moments passed and the only sound to be heard was the soft clopping of the horses upon the earth and the gentle rustling of their tails. Finally, Reynard seemed like he could bear it no longer and he dared to whisper.

"There's nothing to hear."

However, Sir Bertilak wasn't of the same opinion. He held up a hand to quiet Reynard, and the poet along with the rest of the men fell silent. Their horses came to a halt as Sir Bertilak strained his ears against the silence of the deserted forest. In the distance, there were a few lonely bird calls. Overhead there was the creaking of old dried tree branches against the wind.

But there was something closer. Something faint. Quiet. Barely there. Yet decidedly unsettling.

"I hear a rustle…" whispered Sir Bertilak. "A rattle… A breath… A… snort?"

All at once, there was a monstrous grunt and a nearby pile of brush exploded as a massive boar charged out and pressed down upon Sir Bertilak and his men. But this wasn't any ordinary pig. It was at least three times the weight and height of an normal boar, and a normal boar wasn't exactly small in the first place. This one stood nearly as tall as the horses, but wider by far than all of them. Its great hairy bristling snout was framed by two twisted jagged tusks that protruded out of its foaming mouth.

And, of course, its eyes glowed an unnatural emerald green.

The terrifying beast streaked at them. Sir Bertilak and his men couldn't draw their weapons quick enough.

~   ~   ~

With a quick clean tear, Nelle ripped off a long piece of clean white fabric. Then with her nimble small fingers she wrapped it around Gawain's left biceps. The final bit was the most challenging since it involved tying off the bandage in a way that bound it securely in place while still covering the wounded area. There was also the problem of making sure it wasn't so tight that it cut off crucial blood flow, and yet being careful to see that it wasn't so

161

loose that it might quickly slip away. Over her years as a nurse, Nelle had come to think of her work as a delicate artform similar to the precise calligraphies that she had seen practiced by travelling monks, or the elaborate paper foldings of the strange cultures to the distant mystical east. Now, she took a moment to appreciate the perfectly clean bandage although she knew full well that in mere moments it would begin to sully and never be this pristine again. Nonetheless, as she finished wrapping Gawain's arm, Nelle dipped her chin and allowed herself a slight proud smile that was hers alone to enjoy.

After taking her moment of quiet pride, Nelle rose and began to gather her things with the full intention of leaving. She hadn't said a word to the knight this entire time, and she had no intention to, if she could help it.

However, she was doomed to disappointment, because as she turned to head for the door, Gawain cried, "Wait! Aren't you forgetting something?!"

Instinctively, Nelle dropped her gaze further as she spun back toward him. The truth was that over the past days she had enjoyed her little bits of time with Gawain. She flushed slightly at the sound of his voice and his playful demand. Yet, after their strange interaction the night before, when she had allowed herself to be too comfortable with him and say too much, she had determined to say as little to him as possible. It would simply lead to more questions.

And that would be too dangerous for her.

Her stomach tightened as she tilted her head slightly to Gawain as if to say, What could I possibly have forgotten?

The rugged knight trilled at her in his resonate warm voice, "You didn't give me my protection charm?"

Nelle smiled her mousy wry smile and despite her best efforts she couldn't help but incline her chin upward just a few degrees and share it with the man whose beard was so fascinatingly tangled with charms and trinkets. Remaining just as silent as before, but with her cheeks warming ever so slightly, she sunk back down beside him. Then she carefully traced a circular healing symbol with her index finger that seemed so small against his broad arm. She had learned this particular symbol from a group of gypsies that had stumbled upon her and her family when they were hiding deep in the forests when she was just a small girl. Once she had finished tracing along Gawain's arm, Nelle placed her thumb and smallest finger on the knight's leg and silently whispered a spell she had learned from an old witch. Finally, she placed both her palms flat against his wide chest. This time she simply closed her eyes, cleared her mind, and prayed. She felt the heat in her hands flow into his heart.

Then she tensed herself as she bore the stab of cold that seized her entire body for a brief instant.

Her attempt to keep her discomfort as small and imperceptible as possible appeared to have been successful. Gawain didn't seem to have noticed anything as he said, "There. Bring on The Green Knight,"

At the simple mention of the name, Nelle's soft smile faltered. This time, Gawain noticed.

"That was just a joke," said Gawain ruffled by her sudden silence.

Partially from his abashed response and partially from the unnatural chill she had just endured, Nelle's throat went dry. She had always tried to help people in her admittedly small ways, and now here before her sat a man who truly needed her help. Needed it so badly that he didn't know how much he needed it. And she was terrified to give it.

With slightly trembling hands, Nelle fumbled into a pocket in her apron and drew out a tiny tear-drop shaped silver amulet. It was dull and unimpressive compared to the sparkling Roman coin that dangled from Gawain's hair. Her amulet was nothing when placed beside the shark's tooth hanging from the end of a long thin braid. Nelle reached for a handful of Gawain's tangled hair and hoped that he'd accept her gift without question, and that his more impressive talismans would keep it hidden and safe.

But as she tried to weave it into his locks, Gawain grabbed her shaking fingers and asked, "What are you doing? What's that?"

She stayed silent.

"Nelle, talk to me," he demanded.

Still she refused.

"Say something!" he shouted as he gripped her wrists and shook her. "What is wrong with you? What do you know that you're not telling me? What is this thing?"

The words almost slipped from her mouth as she whisper, "It's for The Green Knight."

The bold gregarious man seemed to be struck silent for a moment as he stared at Nelle's tiny unimpressive amulet. Finally he asked, "What is it? Where did you get it?"

But she had already said more than she had meant to and now she simply asked him, "Just trust me."

Once again she reached for a lock of his hair, but once again Gawain pushed her hands away as he said softly, "I can't accept that."

"Please..." she pleaded. "It could make your death easier!"

Gawain pushed her hands away anyway. The nurse and her patient sat in stony silence for a long moment before Gawain said, "I won't take it. I'd just have to give it to Sir Bertilak by the end of the day anyway. It'd be hard to deny something that was plain on my face."

Nelle's face dropped and she whispered sadly.

"I just don't want to see you suffer," she said. "You seem so brave. So strong. So good."

"I'm not that good," said Gawain. "I've done many things that I'm not proud of. I'm here in the hope that I might make them right again. But I have to do it the right way."

"How can you be so courageous?" she asked. "Even in the face of your own certain doom."

"I think you would be too."

"No," Nelle said with slight shake of her head as she lowered her eyes again. "I don't have your courage."

"You're built to help people," said Gawain. "I see it in you every time you've been here with me. I see the longing in your eyes when you see the suffering of the people around you."

Once again, Nelle was struggling to find words.

As if he sensed it, Gawain leaned in to implore her, "Nelle, you know more than you're telling me. I promise to help you with anything that's happening here. But you have to help me first. What's going on?"

Nelle felt the familiar grip on her stomach. Here was her chance to make a difference. She could do something more than just the tiny tears of cloth and the delicate tracing of symbols. But it would cost her. If she helped Gawain and all the others, she was sure it would lead to pain and despair that she could barely imagine.

Despite all this, Nelle steeled her nerves and lifted her head to look Gawain in the eyes. As she locked her gaze on him, she noticed him pause for just a moment and she knew that he was taken aback by her eyes. One blue.

And one green.

She opened her mouth ever so slightly, prepared to reveal all her dark secrets, when another voice broke the silence from behind her.

"Nelle?"

With a burst of shock, the nurse twisted her head to find Lady Bertilak in the doorway. Suddenly all of her courage deserted her.

Gawain was one thing. The lady of the castle was another. In a flash, Nelle rose to her feet and raced quickly out the door. She only paused long enough to cast one quick glance at Gawain's arm where the once pristine bandage had already begun to soil beneath its first traces of dust.

~ ~ ~

The most epic battle twixt good and evil raged on and on and ferociously on. Like a clash of pure white sunshine striking through the thickest, most oppressive storm clouds. And the humble wordsmith, Reynard, the champion of words over strength, the meager vessel through which the heavens spoke, was throwing his heart and soul into the struggle.

He was also already trying to compose a poem about it.

If he was being honest, he wished he could turn off his forever-churning mind for a few moments and focus on the charging beast in front of him. Afterall, a boar that was nearly three times the size of a normal boar was the kind of thing that a person really should put all of his focus on. Especially when it was foaming and snorting and charging with the clear intent of ripping his limbs from his body and stomping his pulsing heart in his chest.

But Reynard often had a hard time turning off his thoughts.

As he attempted to create a perimeter to contain the hairy beast, Reynard reminisced not-too-fondly upon his all-too-simple beginnings. Even from a young age, he had always loved words, he marvelled at the unexpected power they could convey, he ached over the awe-inspiring ability to crush souls with their beauty. But

Reynard had the misfortune of being born to a father who couldn't read and could barely even string two words together. An inquisitive, thought-provoking, ever-questioning young boy and his monosyllabic, dullard father. It made for very one-sided conversations.

"Father, why does the sky stretch in forever widening pools of space and imagination?"

"*It's blue.*"

"Father, what makes the softly rippling plains shine with their blades of evergreen?"

"*Grass?*"

"Father, what is the ultimate nature of the grand expansive world and our place in it?"

"*Eat.*"

Inevitably, Reynard's father always fell back to that familiar command. To be fair, despite all of his considerable shortcomings, Reynard was always well fed and healthy. He just wasn't happy. After his meals, he would return to his small room with his small supply of candles and read and reread his small collection of books.

As soon as he was old enough, he packed up the few tattered books that he owned and prepared to journey out into the world and learn about its various wonders. He bid his father a not-so-memorable farewell.

"Father, I must venture out into the great unknown in search of my elusive and possibly terrible destiny."

"*Bye.*"

With that, Reynard left and intended never to return. His life on the road was the glorious rumination of his beleaguered unfulfilling beginnings. He climbed mountains and traversed through streams. He listened to eye-opening, thrilling tales from monks and barmaids alike. And he read. Oh the gods, did he read. He had always known that there was an ocean of books and poems out there, but now that he was able to get his hands on even a small portion of them, he couldn't get enough.

He devoured the Roman plays that chronicled Oedipus, Agamemnon, and Medea. He raced through Homer's epics about Odysseus and Aeneas. He consumed greedily the solemn parables about Samson and Delilah, Daniel and the lion's den, and the glorious rise and fall and rise again of Jesus of Nazareth. These amazing stories of both heart-breaking tragedy and awe-inspiring triumph naturally captured Reynard's imagination, and he sought to add to their ranks. He began his search for the proper subject, the suitable tale, the most thrilling adventure.

And now here he was, fighting side-by-side with a man who had the makings of a legendary hero engaging in a battle with a beast that seemed to have been spat out of the very depths of hell itself.

And all he could think about what was "what is the best word to rhyme with tusks?"

Reynard snapped out of his daze as marveled at the skill with which Sir Bertilak had drawn his bow and let fly a glorious volley of arrows upon the beast. One, two, three, four, five. The reeds of piercing, pointed wood flew strong and true at their target. Yet they did no good. Each of the arrows simply bounced off the boar's twisting tusks or buried themselves uselessly in its hide. All it did was serve to make the massive pig angry.

Suddenly, Reynard watched as the boar turned and charged at his brave lord, Sir Bertilak. Sir Bertilak had meant to meet the charge head on, but his horse had different ideas. The four-legged steed cowered at the last moment, and reared backward onto its hind legs. It was enough to momentarily panic the boar and send it veering off course. However, it was also enough to send Sir Bertilak flying from his saddle and crashing painfully to the ground.

The mighty lord of Hautdesert Castle scrambled to get his bearings, but his bow had slipped from his fingers. A rumbling grunt brought him to his senses, and Sir Bertilak spun to see the boar turning to begin its next and most brutal charge. With a mix of terror and awe, Reynard watched as the boar dug its sharp hooves into the ground and leapt forward at Sir Bertilak who seemed to have no choice but to screw up his face in anticipation of the terrible fate that awaited him.

"My lord!"

In a flash of inspiration that Reynard had never felt before and that he was certain was sent by the heavens above, he flung himself from the relative safety of his own steed. The simple poet flew through the air, and for a brief moment, felt the weightlessness of destiny lifting him up. He drew his dagger. It flashed through the air. He slammed down upon the boar, wrapped his arms around it, and buried the sharp weapon into the beast. It went absolutely, furiously, ferociously, unstoppably mad as it twisted, bit, grunted, and fought with every bit of its considerable strength.

And Reynard's mind finally went clear.

~ ~ ~

Lady Bertilak had just thrown caution to the wind and then correspondingly thrown herself at Sir Gawain. She was barely in the door when she flung her arms around the strong, handsome man with the wild beard and strange accoutrements. It was a desperate move, but Lady Bertilak couldn't deny that she had become a desperate woman.

Her bold gesture had caught Gawain off guard, and she managed to kiss him once on the cheek before he had even known what was happening. But, as she leaned in to kiss him again, fully on the lips, the powerful knight caught her by the wrists and held her back. She struggled against him and tried to embrace him, but he would have none of it.

"Please, Sir Gawain, don't stand on ceremony any longer," she said as tears streamed down her face. "I need you."

But he was the consummate knight through and through as he rebuffed her advances and said, "I can't kiss you, Lady Bertilak. Please, my lady, what has gotten into you? If I might be so bold, you don't seem like the strong lady with whom I battled wolves just two days ago."

His blunt assessment of her brought Lady Bertilak up short. He was quite right, of course. She had always been a brave woman.

More than once, she had put men to shame with her own courage in the face of overwhelming odds. In fact, when she was younger it had become a point of pride for her. As a young girl, she would race against the boys her age and nearly always outstripped them all. She took the most pleasure in beating the cockiest young men, the ones who would've never admitted that a girl could've have beaten them.

Of course, as she grew a bit more mature, her ability to show up the boys had inevitably led to them falling madly in love with her. As much as many of the boys wanted to protest, there was no denying that they were drawn to a strong woman. This allure had given Lady Bertilak the opportunity to travel far and wide as she became the desire of many potential suitors. Men from all over the lands of Briton and the surrounding isles had wished to meet her and seek her hand. When she was still a young impressionable lady, she had been happy to journey to all of the far away places, but time and time again, Lady Bertilak had found herself to be disappointed. All of the men simply wanted to possess her. They might've been drawn to her strength, but not so that they could embrace it. They liked the idea of stamping it out and being the one to finally tame her.

However, not a one of them was able to succeed.

As Lady Bertilak grew into a woman she learned how to not only be physically strong but also clever and, since she was smart enough to use the skills available to her, beguiling. Where once she had simply been happy to physically outmatch the boys who desired her. Now she had more tricks up her lovely sleeves, and she happily used them to show a thing or two to the men who wished only to control her.

A powerful military commander had attempted to tame her.

She had him dashing naked and embarrassed in front of his laughing troops.

A handsome sailor had tried to make her his next conquest.

She had seen to it that he felt the wrath of his other wives and the mermaids too.

The handsome Sir Bertilak showered her with praise and love. *And everything changed.*

For her entire life, Lady Bertilak had only met men who seemed to want to possess her for her beauty and then take the opportunity to stamp out her spirit. Sir Bertilak was different. Certainly, he was just as proud and boastful as many of the other men, but his was a more playful endearing way. He truly loved her and gave her gifts and threw celebrations in her honor. Lady Bertilak was only too happy to take his name. Once they were married, Sir Bertilak had invited her strength along with him on his many hunting expeditions. It seemed as though she had finally found someone who respected and honored her strength.

Now she finally felt that her strength wasn't enough.

Sir Bertilak had lost control of his lands. All around them, things were crumbling and turning to despair. Lady Bertilak had intended to stand beside her husband, but then a brave knight arrived and her resolve crumbled. Upon meeting Gawain, Lady

Bertilak had realized that here was another great man, one who could perhaps put even Sir Bertilak to shame, and Lady Bertilak couldn't help but admit that she wanted him. She didn't want to simply watch the destruction of Hautdesert Castle as the dutiful wife of Sir Bertilak. She also wanted to have Sir Gawain.

And he had rejected her.

Lady Bertilak wiped away her tears as she said, "Then you don't have to kiss me, Sir Gawain. I thought it might make it easier for you, but I'm not asking for that. Please! Please, just get me out of here…"

Then she buried her face in Gawain's strong arms and sobbed.

"It's going to be all right…" Gawain said as he softly stroked her hair with his rough hands. "You'll see, I'm going to face the Green Knight. And I'm going to stop him. Then you and everyone here can live in peace once more."

Lady Bertilak raised her tear-streaked face and looked into the noble yet wild face of Sir Gawain and she shook her head.

"No. If you face him, you will die," she said.

"Everyone keeps saying that…" said Gawain with a hint of frustration coming through.

"My husband cannot stop him," said Lady Bertilak. "Dozens of other men could not stop him. And you cannot hope to either."

She watched as her words pierced into Sir Gawain and the color and hope drained out of his mighty face. It had been a cruel thing to say, but she had come to learn that this was a cruel world.

Yet she hoped to offer Gawain a ray of light as she said, "But we can escape."

She ran her soft fingers through his ragged beard and played with the dangling shark's tooth and strange foreign amulets. This was the real reason that she had come here today. All her life, she had taken pleasure in her strength and her ability to do without men. But she needed this one.

"You and I can run away from here," Lady Bertilak said. "We can escape from him. You could keep us safe. And I could keep us happy."

Once again, she leaned in and kissed Gawain. But this time it was on the lips. This time it was soft and tender and beautiful. It seemed to have taken him off guard, but this time, Gawain accepted it.

She had kissed him twice, and now she could see that Gawain's resolve was crumbling too.

"Will you do it? Will you leave here with me?" she dared to ask in a voice that was barely above a whisper.

"What about the others?" Gawain asked. "All the people here? The ones who live in the castle? The ones who live in the surrounding lands and count on it for their protection and livelihood?"

"You've heard them. They're all fools. Cheering on my husband as this place crumbles around them," she said bitterly. "I'm sorry to say it, but they are already lost. My husband has seen to that. But we don't have to be. We could live a long, happy life together."

Once again, she petted his beard with her soft hand as she willed him to be her savior and just say 'yes.'

"Where would we go?"

"We can go back to your home," Lady Bertilak said.

"Then the Green Knight will surely take my lands," said Gawain shaking his head.

"Then we'll go somewhere else," said Lady Bertilak. "We'll stay on the move. He'll never find us. But we'll have each other."

She leaned in to kiss him once more. Her soft lips were close to his and she could feel the stray hairs on his beard tickling her smooth chin. She moved in close and saw him close his eyes. Lady Bertilak did the same as she prepared to seal her escape with one last kiss. But, at the last moment, she felt those familiar hands grasping her wrists once again and gently pushing her away. Lady Bertilak opened her eyes to see Gawain's sad pained expression.

"No. I won't run. I'm going to face him," he said. "I'll let him kill me, if I have to. But I'll keep my end of my bargain."

"You won't save me?" was her last desperate request.

"Not like this."

All her life, men had thrown themselves at Lady Bertilak, but now the one man that she had needed and wanted more than any other was refusing her.

"I thought you were a brave knight," she said quietly and bitterly, "But you're not a knight. You're just a coward."

The words stung at Gawain as he shot back, "I'm not a coward..."

"Yes, you are! A coward fights a losing battle out of pride and-"

"This isn't pride..." he argued.

"Yes, it is!" she said, cutting off his argument, and suddenly the words were spilling out of her. She had always tried to keep a cool head, but now it felt so good to lash out as she cried, "You're trying to prove once again that you're the mighty Sir Gawain, willing to die for no reason except for the glory of being able to say you had the courage to march to your end when no one else would. That's not being brave. That's not being righteous. That's being foolish."

"That's doing the right thing," he said simply.

The lady and the knight stared at each other and saw their own dooms reflected in the others' face. The moment lingered until it was broken by a shout that ripped through the air.

"Sir Gawain! I have your gifts for the day..."

Lady Bertilak recognized the voice as that of her husband. But there was something she didn't recognize. There was a soft tremble, a slight catch. She watched as Gawain rose and moved over toward the hole in his wall and looked out. For her part, Lady Bertilak stood a few feet behind Gawain so that she could observe her husband, but she knew he wouldn't be able to see her.

The tall powerful form of Sir Bertilak stood beside the small wagons that he had always brought along on the hunt so that he could cart back the kill. Today it seemed to strain under the weight of two carcasses. One was absolutely massive, so large that it made the other look small and sad beside it. Lady Bertilak watched as her husband flipped back a dirty soiled blanket from the first mound to reveal the dead body of an enormous boar. Then a moment later, Sir Bertilak removed a simple white sheet that had covered the second dead thing, and she understood the catch in her husband's voice.

The body of Reynard laid motionless and peaceful beside the beast that had brought him down.

Lady Bertilak looked to the men in her life, Gawain at the gaping hole in the wall, Sir Bertilak down below, and she saw the two proud men both sagging in despair. And she knew that she wasn't the only one whose strength had failed.

~ ~ ~

CHAPTER 15

A Farewell Feast

The cold gray day gave way to a freezing black night, and a third bonfire was lit on the grounds of Hautdesert Castle. It blazed powerfully as it fed on the piles of wood that had been collected from the scores of dried and dying trees of the surrounding lands. Now the flames rose high and tickled the endless expanse of night sky above. Crackles of fire popped and broke away to join the twinkling stars overhead, and for just an instant, the small embers of the fire glowed in the sky and were indistinguishable from the shining jewels of space before the tiny bits of flame went out and died alone.

Once again men, women, and children had gathered around the towering fire. They had come out of the castle. They had come from the nearby farms that had recently become barren and lifeless. They had come with the hope of forgetting their troubles for another night as they joined friends for a feast of food and wine.

But there was no joy this night.

At one end of the fire, a huge mound of dirt lay still and peaceful. Beside it Sir Bertilak stood with his back to the earth as he looked upon the crowd who had gathered there. He could see his wife, his nurse, and the other men from his usual hunting party. He could see his valets, cooks, and maids. He could see Sir Gawain

179

dressed in what were surely meant to be his most respectful trinkets, beads and talismans.

But Sir Bertilak couldn't see Reynard.

His best friend was behind him now. Buried beneath that mound of cold, unforgiving earth.

"Reynard was a good friend. He was a good man. He was a... poet," said Sir Bertilak as he raised a glass. "While he might not have had time to compose a poem that would withstand the test of time, his memory shall stay with us forever."

With that, the lord of the castle lifted his voice and sang a funeral dirge for his fallen friend:

The new year birthed
On a cold dark winter's night,
It took first breath
Under an icy light
The white snow lay,
That new birth day,
And melted down
Beneath the youngling sprite.

The new year child
Stumbled through the spring,
It found its feet
While butterflies took wing,
It warmed and slept,
It laughed and wept,
The childhood passed

180

With roses and kite string.

The new year grew
Through summer into man,
The warm sun shone
O'er the year's longest span,
The days stretched long,
Grown tall and strong,
And left too quick
As through its time it ran.

The new year slowed
In brisk cool autumn's wind,
And sunsets dimmed
Wise eyes that seldom sinned,
The gold leaves fell,
Time cast its spell,
And wrinkles crept
Along the well-lived skin.

The winter's peace
Returned to greet the year,
With snow white smile
And single frozen tear,
The two embraced,
Close interlaced,
And then made way

181

To welcome the next year.

As Sir Bertilak finished his funeral dirge, he fell into silence for a long moment. All around him, everyone gazed upon the mound of earth that was once his friend. Many of them knew Reynard in passing. Only a few knew him well. But the loss of his presence was certainly felt now. After a few silent moments, Sir Bertilak raised his cup and everyone followed his example.

"To Lord Reynard," said Sir Bertilak as his eyes began to shine with tears.

Dozens of voices resounded and echoed the toasts, "To Lord Reynard!"

Then all the cups were pressed to their owners' lips and the tribute of wine, memory and remorse was complete. Once again, Sir Bertilak scanned through the crowd and he was pleased to see the solemn faces on all the people who had gathered there. He felt that it was a fitting final audience for the man who had always sought to inspire and entertain those around him.

But then Sir Bertilak noticed that the eyes of his wife were especially puffy and red. From the look of things, she had been crying for quite some time. For a moment, Sir Bertilak took solace in the fact that his wife shared in his grief. Unfortunately, he quickly realized that her attention wasn't on the funeral mound.

She seemed to have eyes only for Sir Gawain.

As the night's revelries commenced, it was a decidedly more subdued affair than in the past. The boar that had recently caused so much pain, had now been roasted and served to all in attendance. Everyone had accepted their share, and Sir Bertilak hadn't even noticed the usual balking at the source of the feast. Wine had been poured for all who wished it.

But there was no music. There was no laughter. There was not even much conversation.

Amidst the solemn banquet, Sir Bertilak approached Gawain.

"I gave you what came to me today, Sir Gawain," said Sir Bertilak, his eyes burning with a furious gaze. "Now it's your turn. What have you for me?"

"I have nothing to help you, Sir Bertilak," Gawain said.

The knight seemed to be seeking a conciliatory tone, but it only raised Sir Bertilak's passion as he insisted, "Give me what's mine, good sir knight. That I might ease my sadness."

But Gawain stood firm, "Nothing can relieve your grief, my lord."

"What have you got?!" cried Sir Bertilak, as certainty built inside him that Gawain was holding back on him.

"Just let it be," growled Gawain as his frustration also grew.

Not being able to stand his anger and grief any longer, and desperately needing something to strike out against, Sir Bertilak shoved Gawain hard. The knight didn't return the blow and stood strong against the push.

"We had an agreement. Give me what's mine!" demanded Sir Bertilak.

For a long moment, Gawain just glared at Sir Bertilak, but then all of sudden, Gawain grabbed Bertilak by the shoulders and pulled him in for a quick kiss on the cheek. One kiss. Sir Gawain then grumbled as he seemed to struggle with a decision before quickly giving Sir Bertilak a quick kiss on the other cheek.

Two kisses.

That was all that Gawain had for him. It was silly. It was absurd. It was a child's game between two grown men who had experienced lifetimes of loss and struggle. The quick sign of affection burned on Bertilak's cheeks.

"Who?" asked Sir Bertilak.

"Not the deal," replied Gawain.

The two men stared each other down. Daring each other to make the next move. Neither was sure what would happen next. And secretly, Sir Bertilak wished for an explosion, an epic duel, a fight to the death. Anything to help him control the furious emotions that roiled inside of him. But then Sir Bertilak broke down as hot tears poured down his handsome, quivering face. He buried himself in Gawain's arms.

And Gawain held the sobbing man, not sure what else to do.

~   ~   ~

CHAPTER 16

The Poet's Last Song

As if to mock the many mourners in Hautdesert Castle, the sun shone brightly the next morning and even succeeded for a short time in turning the bleak colorless skies into a wide expanse of clear blue eternity. Gawain had risen with the sun, and was pleased to feel like his old self once more. He had quickly dressed and ventured out of his room to find the castle to still be a solemn quiet deserted place.

Eventually, he had journeyed out into the grounds and, for the first time of his stay, he found the stables. Despite the early hour, Gawain stumbled upon Sir Bertilak and his hunting party as they were preparing to ride out. Each of them bore swords on their hips. Sir Bertilak had his bow and quiver slung over his shoulder. Their horses were loaded up for another full day's excursion of tempting fate.

"Let me ride with you today, Bertilak," offered Gawain as he approached the lord of the castle.

"Go back to bed, Sir Gawain," said Sir Bertilak.

"It's dangerous out there," said Gawain. "You could use all the help you can get. Your people need you here. I'm not entirely sure you should be risking yourself."

"I'm well up to this task."

185

"And I'm well up for the hunt," said Gawain. "At least, let me go with you. You need another man."

"I said stay here!"

Gawain was taken aback by the sudden outburst of Sir Bertilak. The knight had originally found Sir Bertilak to be an uncommonly good man. He was kind and friendly and generous. Now, it seemed as though Bertilak was coming apart at the seams. The ever-present danger had taken its toll and Gawain knew what that could mean in a life or death situation. Gawain had seen men who were too tired or too grieved or too sad to operate correctly. They made mistakes and they got people hurt.

Before Gawain had a chance to argue, however, Sir Bertilak mounted onto his horse and all of his men did the same.

"Sir Bertilak, wait," started Gawain.

But Bertilak cut across him and said, "Our deal stands. I'll see you at the sunset."

And as simply as that, the lord of Hautdesert Castle rode away with his men. Gawain watched as they left the stables, and he watched them gallop past the smoldering ashes in the fire pit that just hours ago had held a towering bonfire.

It may have been a trick of the early morning light, but as Sir Bertilak and his men rode past the fire pit, Gawain thought he saw Reynard's funeral mound pulse ever so slightly. Gawain shook his head, the slight cracks in the pile of earth were certainly there all along.

Once Sir Bertilak was gone, Gawain returned to the stables and found a familiar gray, slightly speckled horse waiting for him.

Ringolet huffed indignantly at Gawain's approach.

"Sorry to have left you here, my friend," said Gawain as he patted Ringolet on the head. "I hope you've been well-treated."

Ringolet neighed and shook his head angrily.

"I said I'm sorry!" cried Gawain. "I didn't mean to leave you here. I wasn't exactly in the best of conditions myself."

As Gawain reached to stroke Ringolet's mane, the horse turned his long head away in order to deny his master the pleasure.

"Stop being a colt! At least you're well rested. And you got some good feeding."

The horse pulled his head even further away.

"Don't worry, I'm ready to get out of here too," said Gawain before he added, "But I won't pretend that some things won't be harder to leave than others."

Ringolet blinked at his master.

"You see her too, don't you?"

Both knight and horse turned to a dark corner of the quiet stables to see the nurse silently stepping forward.

"You don't ever have to hide from me," Gawain said to Nelle.

Quietly and with her head bowed as usual, Nelle approached Gawain as she said, "I never really hide. It's just that people usually don't notice me."

"Their mistake."

"You'd be surprised what I can pick up while the men are preparing to leave. All sorts of little secrets and treasures," explained Nelle.

"Is that why you're here? To lift a spare coin off Bertilak? Or to overhear a secret from one of his men?" asked Gawain.

"No, I'm here to see you," said Nelle, and Gawain felt his breathing restrict ever so slightly in curious anticipation, "I'm here to tell you to go. Right now. Don't tell anyone, don't say good-bye. Just go."

"Why would I do that?"

"Darkness is coming here," said Nelle. "It's inevitable. I don't want you to be here when it comes."

"Maybe I can help," suggested Gawain. "Has everyone forgotten that I am, forgive my immodesty, an extremely accomplished knight?"

"It won't be enough this time," said Nelle. "This place is doomed. Nothing can save it."

"Maybe I can. Maybe I can save you all."

Nelle just smiled. A small, sad smile.

"No. It doesn't matter what you do. You won't be able to save me."

"I'm going to go and face the Green Knight. I'm going to take up his challenge. I believe I can save you. All of you," said Gawain.

"You can go and die, if you like," said the kind little nurse as she placed a tiny hand against Gawain's great bearded cheek, "I won't try and stop you. Just don't do it here. Don't make me watch. Don't make me feel it."

"Feel it?" asked Gawain as he looked at her with confusion. But she simply looked away, prompting the mighty knight to say, "What if I scooped you up, and we ran away from here together?"

This seemed to genuinely shock Nelle as she asked, "Why would you want to run away with me?"

Gawain seemed genuinely shocked by her genuine shock, "Why wouldn't I?"

Gawain brushed aside her thin, slightly frazzled hair. He found it lovely. He lifted her small downturned face. He found it beautiful. But as he leaned in to kiss her, she pushed him away.

There wasn't a tear in her eyes, there wasn't a quiver in her voice, but her words tore into Gawain as Nelle simply asked, "Please... Just go..."

The noble knight accepted his lady's request. He turned and left.

~   ~   ~

Once more, Sir Bertilak and his men rode through the forest on the hunt. Their weapons were at the ready. Their horses were rested and well-fed. They were ready to do their duty and seek out any threats to their lands and their people. However, none of them were at their best. Their hearts were no longer in the fight. All of the men were quiet this day. No talking. No joking. No smiles.

Not one of them noticed a shadow hanging over them.

They scanned the cold hard terrain for any sign of enemies.

The shadow moved.

This time, Sir Bertilak stopped. He raised his hand, and his men halted. They all looked around for any sign of an enemy, and they each strained their ears against the eerie creaking of the dead tree branches against the wind.

"...Fall back..."

Sir Bertilak looked around at each of his men. At first, he had hoped that he had merely imagined the faint whisper. However, the pale looks of disquiet on everyone's faces confirmed Sir Bertilak's dread. They all heard it too.

"...Attack..."

More whispers. More looking. More nothing.

"...Hack..."

Sir Bertilak finally looked up and his heart froze at what he saw. Reynard perched up in the branches above him. But the dead man's clothes were filthy from his burial mound. His limbs were twisted at odd angles to help him balance precariously in the trees. His face was pale and bluish.

And his eyes glowed an emerald green.

"...The brave and righteous Bertilak..."

The Undead Man sprung from the tree, and fell upon his former friends with a brutal attack that meant to shatter their bones and break their hearts.

~ ~ ~

Gawain only intended to return to the castle for a few short moments. It didn't take him long to collect his belongings. It also didn't take him long to gather up the pieces of his painted armor. Finally, it took the least time of all to tidy up the few items that were left in the room. He turned to leave when he heard a soft voice say,

"You're going?"

Gawain found Lady Bertilak lurking once again in his doorway. He realized that he might be stuck longer than he intended.

"I have to go," said Gawain. "I will do the brave thing. I'm going to find The Green Knight as soon as I can. I'll keep my bargain. And, maybe, I can free this land from yours."

"You may wish for that to be the case," said Lady Bertilak with sadness in her voice, "But it's not true. You'll face him. Perhaps bravely. But he'll defeat you. And it will all have been for nothing."

"I don't think so," explained Gawain. "In all the readings I've done. In all the places I've visited, no one has ever had the courage to stand up to him."

"Because he's certain to win," she said.

"No, that's just what he wants everyone to think," said Gawain. "So he spreads rumors of his immense strength. He builds legends of it. He gets children to sing rhymes about it. And then everyone is too scared to show up for their rematch. But, I think, if I stand up to him, his power will break."

"But how far will you have to go to keep your end of the bargain?"

"As far as I have to."

"Even if he demands that, to show your courage, you must die?" she asked in a small voice.

Gawain nodded, and immediately Lady Bertilak's eyes began to tear up. He was relieved to find, however, that she didn't try to stop him this time. Instead she did something very strange. Gawain watched as the lovely blonde lady of the castle, drew a thin, nearly transparent green sash out of her bodice.

"This sash has been passed down by the women in my family for generations," she said as she pressed the silky scarf into Gawain's hands.

But Gawain forced it away as he said, "No, I can't take this."

"It has powerful protections," insisted Lady Bertilak. "Wear it beneath your armor. Or tuck it into the toe of your boot, if you wish. It will fit almost anywhere. It can keep you safe."

"Why didn't you give this to your husband when his rematch loomed?" asked Gawain.

Lady Bertilak sputtered for a moment before finally replying, "I would have, but he didn't even go to his rematch. Maybe it can still help you."

But now Gawain's thoughts were on the lord of the castle as he repeated, "I cannot accept that. I promised your husband that anything I received in this castle that would give back to him. It wouldn't be the right thing to do to take that."

"He'll never know," said Lady Bertilak, "Please, you saved my life. Maybe I can repay the favor."

Once again, she placed the sash into Gawain's hand, and this time she forced him to close his fingers around it. Simply having it in his hands gave a Gawain feeling of warmth and safety. He felt the smooth, cool silk of the scarf between his fingers and he relaxed ever so slightly for what felt like the first time in years. He nodded.

"Thank you."

~   ~   ~

The Undead Reynard was more brutal and fearsome than the man ever was in life. He leapt from one man to another and his powerful blows made the men crumble beneath his brutality. The battle had raged for only minutes and Reynard had already left most of the men dead in his wake. He had smashed their skulls or crushed their chests or shattered their bones. Sir Bertilak and his hunting party were nearly helpless against their foe. Their swords managed to cut Reynard's bluish flesh, but it gave him no pain. It failed to slow him even a little bit. With startling speed and strength, Reynard pounced upon Sir Bertilak's final loyal follower. The green-eyed undead Reynard slammed his prey into a tree, and even though the man was larger and heavier than Reynard, Reynard easily lifted him up into the air by the throat.

Sir Bertilak alone had managed to survive the onslaught thus far. He had been the first to attack Reynard, but Sir Bertilak's sword was no use. Reynard had caught the blade in his bare hand and bent it with his unnatural impossible strength. Then the undead Reynard had struck Sir Bertilak with such force as the brave man had never felt before. He had felt his ribs crack as he flew nearly twenty feet and painfully slammed to the hard frozen ground. In the moments it took Sir Bertilak to regain his wits, he had heard the screams of terror of his fellow men and he had seen vague blurs of red as Reynard flung himself upon the others and silenced them forever.

Now Sir Bertilak fumbled to fix an arrow into his bow in a last desperate attempt to bring Reynard down and to save his final friend. Sir Bertilak fired his arrow and it buried itself deep into Reynard's back.

But the dead man didn't so much as flinch.

He looked over his shoulder with his menacing, green glowing eyes fixed upon Sir Bertilak and then, almost casually, he snapped the neck of the man he held in the air.

"Please, my friend," gasped Sir Bertilak. "Cease this madness!"

Reynard tossed the dead body aside as if it was a rag doll that he had lost interest in. Then he sprang impossibly high into the sky at Sir Bertilak. The undead man crashed down from the air and pinned Sir Bertilak to the ground. Over their friendship, Sir Bertilak and Reynard had sparred several times. and it was true, Reynard had been fairly good with a sword and bow. But Reynard had never been particularly imposing and it was mostly because he had never been a man of strength. However, now Sir Bertilak struggled with all of his considerable might yet was barely able to stir more a few inches, and it seemed as if Reynard was barely trying at all.

Reynard's hands closed around Sir Bertilak's neck, and Sir Bertilak felt their icy touch against his skin and he ached under the impossible strength of Reynard's terrible grip. Even though his vision was already beginning to blur around the edges, Sir Bertilak saw one of his men's swords a few feet away. He stretched with all of his might. His fingertips brushed the handle.

"I'm sorry, my friend," said Sir Bertilak, sacrificing the little air he had left in his burning lungs for his lost friend.

But Reynard's grimace was cold and merciless.

Sir Bertilak grasped hold of the sword. With all his might, he shoved Reynard backward with his left hand and swung the sword in his right. Reynard's death grip slackened. A moment later, Reynard's headless body fell backward.

Heaving in exhaustion, Sir Bertilak sat up to see the lifeless bodies of not only Reynard but of all his faithful men. He had won this battle.

Yet all was lost.

~ ~ ~

Gawain tucked the sliver of green into his glove then gathered up all of his things once more. As he balanced his helmet under his arm, he looked back to Lady Bertilak who had been watching him all along. She seemed to share his relief over the green sash.

"Thank you," Gawain said with a slight respectful nod. "I won't fail you and your people."

Then he went to pass Lady Bertilak but she held up one hand and she slightly moved to fill the doorway. Gawain paused for a second as he saw Lady Bertilak shake her head, and it was as if she was talking herself into something. Then she stepped boldly toward Gawain and pressed her lips against his. Even if he had wanted to stop her, Gawain's arms were full with all of his meager belongings. Besides, he didn't want to stop her. He felt the delicious warmth spreading out into his fingertips, down into his toes, curling through his spine. The unexpected gesture caused him to stumble backward ever so slightly, it even made him slightly weak in the knees. What did he care? The world as he knew it was confused and broken and headed for its end. Why shouldn't he enjoy this one moment of comfort?

The moment passed, and as they broke apart, Gawain heard her soft whisper.

"For luck."

A small smile curled across his lips. But it too wouldn't last.

"GAWAIN!"

The roaring angry shout snapped Gawain out of his momentary state of bliss, and he spun to make sense of it. He hadn't realized that in the heat of their embrace, Gawain and Lady Bertilak had stumbled directly into the center of the room. They were now in full view of anyone who might look in through the gaping hole in the side of the castle.

They were now in full view of Sir Bertilak.

Gawain looked out the hole in the wall, and saw the lord of the castle leaping off of his horse. Behind the horse was a wagon filled with what appeared to be a stack of bodies. Sir Bertilak didn't seem to be concerned with that now as he left the horse and wagon behind and charged toward the castle. Vaguely, Gawain noticed that Lady Bertilak slipped away in her shame and surprise. Gawain had no intention of doing that. He had never been a man to back down and he wasn't going to now either. Instead of turning and running and sputtering excuses, the knight strode out of his room. He descended the stairs. He emerged through the front gates of the crumbling castle.

And he met the furious lord head on.

"What have you got for me today, Sir Gawain?" said Sir Bertilak in a low tone although his voice was shaking with fury.

"You don't understand what you just saw," said Gawain.

"What have you got for me?!" shouted the lord.

"Nothing…"

"I have six dead men for you," stated Sir Bertilak with a deranged laugh as he pointed back toward the wagon with its stack of covered bodies. "And you've got nothing for me?!"

Gawain gritted his jaw. He didn't like feeling this way. In the few short days that he had been around Hautdesert Castle, he had learned to respect Sir Bertilak. But he had also seen that the lord of the castle had taken leave of his duties and lost control of the place. The man standing before Gawain now was deranged and furious, and Gawain bitterly knew that he was at least somewhat responsible.

"Have you no honor?!" spat Bertilak.

Then and there, Gawain made a decision. If Sir Bertilak wanted what was owed to him, then Gawain would hold up his end of the bargain. He took out that green sash that had been given to him only moments before.

And Gawain threw Sir Bertilak's wife's sash to the ground.

Sir Bertilak barely paused before taking a swing at Gawain. Gawain felt the knuckles collide with his jaw, and he came to appreciate Sir Bertilak once more. The man could hit. He knew how to throw a punch. He knew how to dole out pain. But Gawain knew how to take it. Even as he felt his own teeth digging into the flesh of his cheek, Gawain stood strong. He spat out the little bit of blood and looked Sir Bertilak in the eye once more.

"I won't fight you," said Gawain.

Sir Bertilak hit him again. Gawain took it again.

"Fight back!"

"No."

Another swing from Sir Bertilak. Another taste of copper in the mouth of Gawain.

"Hit me!" shouted Sir Bertilak as he reared back his arm again.

"I won't," said Gawain as he took the vicious blow.

Sir Bertilak wouldn't stop. He hit Gawain again and again and again and again. Eventually, Gawain fell to his knees, but still he took the beating. His mantra to "Just get up" fled from his mind. He deserved this. He'd earned this for a lifetime of foolish prideful decisions that put others in danger. Gawain collapsed. But Sir Bertilak kept hitting. Over and over and more and more. Gawain's world was full of pain, the darkness had seeped in, and it was all nearly over.

But, finally, Sir Bertilak stopped.

And Sir Bertilak dropped down to the ground beside Gawain. After a long moment, Gawain managed to sit up.

"I owed you that," said Gawain through lips that were already starting to swell along with every other bit of his face. "I admit I deserved it."

Sir Bertilak nodded.

"And tomorrow at dawn, I'll go," Gawain told him.

Again, Sir Bertilak simply nodded.

"But, first, let me help you with your men. I owe you that too."

~ ~ ~

There was no feast. No celebration. No food or wine or music. But there was a fire.

A large funeral pyre stacked with the bodies of Sir Bertilak's men burnt savagely hot and consumed the fallen warriors. At Sir Bertilak's side, Gawain was cleaned up, but Sir Bertilak still felt a flush of a cold pleasure at the fact that Gawain didn't look so good. The massive beard and long hair did a fairly good job of hiding most of the knight's bruises, but Sir Bertilak could still see a swollen lip, a cut forehead, and a purplish mass around the eyes. Maybe it was childish of him to take even a small bit of solace from the knight's pain, but Sir Bertilak needed whatever wins he could take right now. And besides, his fist hurt pretty bad too.

"I'm the only one left," said Sir Bertilak as he watched the tall fire burn. "How can I possibly hope to defend my lands now?"

"Maybe I can help you with that," said Gawain.

Sir Bertilak looked into Gawain's slightly bloodshot eyes.

199

"I'm going to ride out in the morning to meet The Green Knight," Gawain continued. "I'll ask him to take me, and spare you and your people. Maybe if he puts all his focus on me, I can get him to leave you alone."

"You'll sacrifice yourself for us?" asked Sir Bertilak quietly and, although the knight didn't know it, mostly to himself. Secretly, Sir Bertilak was forming a plan.

"I will if I can."

There was a long moment of silence, and then Sir Bertilak nodded as he made up his mind to pursue his dark course of action.

"You really aren't an unimpeachable hero, are you?" said Bertilak.

"Not exactly. No…"

Once again they fell into silence, as the knight and the lord of the crumbling castle gazed into the fire's destructive heat.

"At first light, I'll ride out with you," said Sir Bertilak. "I'll take you to Old Swythamley. And point you toward the Green Knight's Chapel."

"Thank you," Gawain said with a slight bow of his head. "However my duel turns out, one way or another, I hope it'll improve your fortunes."

Sir Bertilak nodded again. He was sure that Gawain would improve his fortunes and the fortunes of those who were loyal to him. He was quite sure. Although, it wouldn't be in the way that the knight had presumed. Maybe it wasn't the proper behavior of the lord of a castle, but… At this point, what did Sir Bertilak have to lose?

And with that, Sir Bertilak turned and walked away, leaving Gawain to face the fire alone.

~   ~   ~

CHAPTER 17
Bertilak's Plan

The next morning, Gawain awoke before dawn and felt like himself for the first time in months. Almost inexplicably, he felt strong and limber and fresh. And he craved danger, heroics and adventure. For a full year now, he had teetered on the brink of nerves and anxiety, but today offered the hope of freedom from that. As he dressed himself in his familiar dented, faintly painted armor, Gawain cast his mind back to his first battle with the Green Knight and how all of this began. As he wove some trinkets and talismans into his hair and beard he felt a flush of excitement that it a was all about to come to an end. And Gawain was eager to find out how. Like hearing a story, even one he suspected would resolve itself badly, Gawain couldn't help but want to get to the thrilling conclusion and see how it would end.

He found Sir Bertilak suited up and ready to go down in the stables. Ringolet too, the faithful steed, was fed and rested and ready to depart. The two men mounted their horses in silence and, although they seemed to have a found a mutual respect and wary acceptance of one another, it was clear that any friendship that had been there was over. Gawain shrugged to himself, it wouldn't be the only thing that ended that day.

As they slowly trotted out of the stables, Gawain caught a glimpse of a tiny sweet face hidden in her usual corner. Nelle had come to see him off. Not wanting to potentially betray her secrets to the master of the castle, Gawain inclined his head ever so slightly to her in a gesture of fond farewell. There were many people that Gawain had come to like around Hautdesert Castle, and many of them would inspire warm memories. But there was only one that he would miss. Nelle raised her eyes to him and smiled that tender wry smile and then faded back into the shadows of the stables.

With that, the mighty Sir Gawain and his great horse were off.

The sun was already creeping higher and higher into the skies as Sir Bertilak led the way silently through the surrounding forest. The horses' hooves clopped loudly upon the hard frozen ground and the multitude of bare tree branches interlocked into a strange almost spiderweb before creaking in the cold breeze, swaying slightly and then reforming again into new strange unsettling patterns. For the first time, Gawain was able to appreciate the stress that Sir Bertilak must've been under for weeks if not months. The forest that they were now traversing was a decidedly unwelcoming place, and Sir Bertilak's hunting party must've been dragged down at least partially by the dour mood that hung all around. Now there was only one man left, and Gawain recognized that Sir Bertilak was thoroughly outmatched by the darkness that surrounded him from all sides and even from above and below. Far from dampening Gawain's mood, however, the cold day and the bleak atmosphere served to strengthen the good knight's resolve. Once again, he saw the challenges that lay ahead of him and he thrilled. Still at this moment, his blood pumped hot in his veins, his heart still swelled in his broad powerful chest, he still had a loyal horse and a true blade at his side.

This was an adventure that any knight would've died for.

And there was every likelihood that Gawain would.

Eventually, Sir Bertilak and Gawain emerged from the other end of the dead forest and two distant mountains came clearly into focus against the gray skies. Sir Bertilak led Gawain up to the edge of a ravine, and Gawain looked down the steep rocky slope down to a small stream below. Sir Bertilak pointed along the stream as it snaked slightly west toward the mountains.

"Follow the ravine until it reaches the crest of those mountains," said Sir Bertilak as he gestured to the place where the two mountains were separate.

Gawain took it all in. The mountains and the dark shadowy place that separated them.

"In the shadow of the mountains, at the end of the ravine, you'll find his chapel," finished Sir Bertilak.

"Thank you, Sir Bertilak," said Gawain not bothering to extend a hand to shake or even pat upon Sir Bertilak's shoulder knowing it wouldn't be welcomed or reciprocated.

"Good luck, Sir Gawain of the court of King Uther Pendragon," said Sir Bertilak without even a slight hint of his former mirth.

However, Gawain mustered a bit of his old swagger and decided to try a simple joke as he boasted, "When I return in an inevitable blaze of glory with the blood of the Green Knight on my sword, I promise to help you rebuild your castle."

"Until then," was all the handsome lord could reply.

With a slight nod to one another, the two men finally separated their paths. Gawain urged Ringolet on, and slowly and carefully, the horse worked his way down the rocky slope of the ravine. Every so often some of the uneven surface would give way and cause a small rock slide, but Ringolet was sure-footed and stable through it all, and Gawain appreciated it in a way that he felt didn't need to be said to his faithful friend.

"Not bad, eh, Ringolet?" said the knight to his horse as they reached the small stream at the bottom of the ravine and began to splash along it.

The horse snuffled at him.

"I'm not saying we should live here," said Gawain, "But this is a place that yearns to be saved. And there's scores of people who need the heroics that only we can provide. Lady Bertilak. Nelle. The people who rely on Hautdesert Castle for safety. It's enough to make your blood boil with pride at the noble service we get to offer. Ah yes, my friend, this is truly a great adven-"

SWOOSH!

The arrow plunged itself into a chink in the back of Gawain's armor and instantly all grand thoughts of heroism, chivalry and adventure were driven from Gawain's mind. The impact of it knocked Gawain off of Ringolet's back as the sharp blinding pain caused him to seize up as he fell. Gawain crashed into the stream face first, with the arrow protruding out of his left flank, just above his hip and just off of his spine. The pain shrieked through his body, and try as Gawain might he couldn't reach the arrow. It had landed deep in just such a way that any movement he attempted only made the pain worse. Every nerve seemed to scream at even the smallest twitch.

Which was made worse by the fact that his face was currently underwater.

The stream was only a few inches deep, but Gawain was quickly realizing that a few inches would easily be enough to drown him. He wrenched his head up, and the slight arching of his neck and back was enough to drive the arrow deeper into the cluster of nerves along his spine. It was excruciating, but Gawain endured it long enough to turn his head and look back to the top of the ravine.

Sir Bertilak gazed down from his high vantage point and lifted his bow to Gawain in a farewell salute. Then the treacherous lord turned his horse and rode away.

And Gawain's face fell back under the stream.

The pain was impossible. It paralyzed his every limb and dulled his mind to any possible options he might have left. The little air he had managed to draw in was quickly disappearing. Any moment now, his reflexes would give way and he would gulp in a lungful of the cold merciless water and that would be the end.

The mighty Sir Gawain... he thought bitterly as he forced himself to clench his mouth shut *...Beaten by a trickle...*

As he summoned the will to hold on for one moment more, and then a moment after that, and then a moment after that, Gawain reflected that this wasn't the way things were supposed to end for him. If he was being honest, Gawain had expected to die today. But not like this. He was going to go out in a blaze of glory against the Green Knight and free the people of Tintagel and Hautdesert Castle, not drown in a few measly inches of dirty water. But now his back roared in pain, and his chest burnt from lack of air, and it was all hopeless. And it was over.

When a mouth bit onto his leg.

Ringolet sunk his teeth into the flesh along Gawain's ankle, just below the calf, just above the foot, and inch by painstaking inch drug Gawain out of the water. Slowly, slowly, slowly, the two of them worked their way out of the water onto the rocky bank. Gawain drew in sputtering coughing painful breaths and he was grateful to be free from the water. But he still couldn't reach the arrow, and Ringolet's teeth wouldn't be much help with that. With another painful twist of his head, Gawain looked at his back and saw the arrow protruding out of him, and he saw the stream of hot blood running out of his armor.

"Thanks... old friend..." muttered Gawain as he cast his eyes up at Ringolet. "Now, get out of here... Go live a long horse life..."

But the loyal horse wouldn't desert his master.

"Would you do what I say for once?!"

The horse shook his head.

"You're a good friend..."

207

So far Gawain's epic adventure was off to a miserable start.

~ ~ ~

Lady Bertilak wandered the halls of her crumbling home. It was hard for her to recognize it as the same beautiful place that she had come to just under a year ago. It was filled with so much promise, so much hope, so much strength. Now it was on the verge of utter ruin, it was almost unbelievable. The lady arrived at the doorway of the room that had been the home of Gawain for the past few days. As she glanced into the now cold empty bed chamber, she felt a longing to see him again, so that they might be able to put an end to some of the strange struggles between them. She didn't have long to dwell on it, however, when familiar shouting rung in through the gaping hole in the wall.

"Everyone! Come out here to the feasting pit!" came the shouting from outside. "Come! I must speak to you all!"

Lady Bertilak's face furrowed in confusion as she recognized the voice of her husband. Yet there was something about the tone and tenor of it that didn't sound like himself. He had gone away early this morning with Sir Gawain and both had made a point of not saying good-bye to her. When she awoke and found that her husband and the secret object of her desire had departed so unceremoniously, she felt a flush of anger at first. But she quickly pushed that aside. She had never been the type of woman who dwelled too harshly upon the approvals or disapprovals of men, not even her husband. The fact that Sir Bertilak had seemed to respect her independent streak was part of what fascinated her about him, and ultimately drawn her into a marriage with him. But now Sir Bertilak seemed to be walking a knife's edge and Gawain was gone. As she dashed along the empty hallway, down the stairs and out into the cold winter's air, Lady Bertilak decided that it might be time to bring a close to this section of her life.

"Come! Come closer!" cried Sir Bertilak.

Men, women, and children stumbled in to hear the words of their leader, and he waved his broad powerful arms to urge them ever closer. But as Lady Bertilak emerged from the castle and took a closer look at her husband, she saw that things weren't as well as he would've had everyone believe. His movements were wild and erratic. His eyes darted nervously all around. His normally easy smile seemed forced and even pained. Lady Bertilak hung toward the back of the crowd to see what Sir Bertilak might do. One way or another, she was certain that things were precariously close to falling apart.

"My friends! I have made a decision!" declared her husband and the forced enthusiasm in his voice caused several faces in the crowd to brighten as they convinced themselves that glad tidings were finally on their way. But they were quickly disappointed. "We're going to run! The hordes of beasts may soon press down upon us! They've been growing stronger and coming closer for weeks now."

Lady Bertilak watched her husband in hesitant confusion. He seemed to have a plan, but he also seemed in no condition to come up with a good plan. She was quickly proven right on both accounts.

"But now, all of us together, men, women and children, have a chance. To run!" he said as he thrust a fist into the air.

His weird disjointed speech, however, didn't have the intended effect. No one cheered him on. No one rallied to his cause. In fact, several people began to jeer.

"But this is our home!" shouted one man from the crowd.

"And it's lost! I'm sorry to say, but it's over here," said Sir Bertilak as he shook his head like a madman. "So we'll gather up all that we can carry and make a run for freedom!"

"We can't outrun the beasts," a woman cried.

"Of course, we can!" laughed Sir Bertilak as if it was the simplest thing in the world. "And I think there will be precious few following us anyway. We can easily fight those off."

"But we don't know how to fight," came another woman's response.

"Come now! Look, even a child can hold a sword. See!"

Sir Bertilak drew his sword and forced it into the hands of a small child that stood near the front of the rapidly souring crowd. The child nearly fell over from the weight of the weapon.

"See! We can make it! Together!"

The crowd was grumbling more and more clearly now yet Sir Bertilak seemed unaware of it as he bounced around from foot to foot as if he was doing a strange dance of encouragement.

"I command you all, to prepare to flee! Everyone will be armed. And then we ride to safety!"

The people were starting to disperse.

"Excellent! Go! Get weapons!" shouted Sir Bertilak. "And get your things! Wonderful! Onward!"

As the people scattered looking more confused than convinced, Lady Bertilak rushed over to her crazed husband.

"What's happened to you?!" she demanded.

"Nothing! Nothing's happened!" he said with a wave of his hand that looked in no way casual.

"You can't honestly expect small children and old women to fight bears and wolves," said the lady.

"And why not?!" asked her husband. "This land has turned against us. There's no place for us here anymore. But we may be able to run for it."

"The Green Knight will come after you."

The crazed look in Sir Bertilak's eyes returned. It was true, Lady Bertilak hadn't been married to him for all that long, but she had never seen him look like this. There was a manic glint as he shook his head.

"I don't think so... I think he'll be busy with bigger fish soon."

"What have you done?" asked Lady Bertilak but then it hit her all at once. "What's happened to Sir Gawain?"

Sir Bertilak smiled wickedly as he said, "Forget about him. He's served his purpose. He'll give us cover while we escape."

The quickly maddening lord actually giggled as if he was a child who had just learned a deliciously naughty secret. Lady Bertilak could barely believe that the once brave man had broken so completely, but as she watched him bite on his lower lip, trying to restrain his glee, it became clear that Sir Bertilak was beaten and gone. The Green Knight had already won. Now the only question was how would things fall apart from here.

Almost in answer, a loud growling noise erupted from the nearby trees. Sir Bertilak, who mere moments ago had been bouncing happily, spun and his face dropped as he saw a massive bear lurch out of the forest and lumber toward them with its teeth bared and its mouth foaming.

And its eyes glowing emerald green.

~ ~ ~

CHAPTER 18

The Nurse's Secret

At the bottom of the ravine, Gawain laid face down in the pebbles that scattered along the bank of the small rambling stream. The great knight who had overcome so many monumental challenges was now collapsed and unconscious. The trickle of blood continued to seep out of his back where Bertilak's arrow protruded. His handsome strong horse nudged and nuzzled his master, but it was no good.

Only Nelle could help him now.

The tiny nurse rushed as quickly as her short slightly uneven legs could carry her down the precariously steep ravine. Her feet slipped and skidded as the loose rocks gave way, but she did her best to steady herself as she hurried to the side of Gawain. She crouched beside him, and Nelle was relieved to hear the faint whisper of a breath coming out of the knight's mouth. He was still alive. And after all Nelle had done to heal the great big lout in the past few days, she intended to keep him that way. At first, she gently shook him. Nothing. So she shook him a little harder. Still not so much as a twitch. She shook him with all of her might. But he was as stubborn as ever, and he insistently laid motionless.

"Sleep through this, you big monstrous baby," she said as she took hold of the shaft of the arrow.

Then with a quick showing of all her strength, Nelle ripped the arrow out of Gawain's back.

That did the trick.

Gawain woke with a furious roar and arched his back in what must of been an intense wave of pain. Yet Nelle just shook her head and sighed as she reminded herself that Gawain considered himself one of the greatest knights in the land. Did he expect that to be painless? The big baby...

"Aaaahh!!" Gawain cried as he wrenched around to look at Nelle with wild rage in his eyes. "What is wrong with you, woman?!"

"I thought you were supposed to be mighty and strong..." she said simply.

Gawain grimaced and touched his back. His hand came away slick with his own hot red blood. He grumbled.

"Excellent... You made the bleeding faster..."

"Just be quiet," she said, feeling just a little under appreciated. She had just woken him up afterall, the least he could do was sound grateful. Then she added under her breath but loud enough for him to hear, "You great whimpering puppy."

Nelle pressed her hands to Gawain's back. Almost immediately, he winced under the pressure. But Nelle knew that there was much worse in store for her. She felt the familiar heat collect from throughout her body, and focus itself in her palms. Then she willed the warmth to pass away from her and into the miserable ungrateful knight. Gawain suddenly emitted a harsh ragged gasp. Nelle barely heard it, however, as a deep unnatural cold swept over her, clouding her vision, plugging her ears, and choking her lungs. She wasn't done yet, though. She forced herself to focus as she drew her mind back to all of the complicated and miraculous things she had learned over her short, painful life. As her deft fingers drew complicated, interlocking symbols along Gawain's gaping wound, Nelle remembered her tiny, gnarled grandmother who had been the first to bestow upon Nelle the teachings that her druid family had cultivated over centuries. Nelle called upon the healing powers of nature itself as she began a delicate dance with the air that flowed in and around her.

A gust of wind blew through. And Gawain was able to breath a little easier.

"How are you doing this?" gasped Gawain.

But Nelle ignored the knight's words, as well as her own considerable pain, and she continued on. Gawain was a nice man, but maybe not the brightest, and Nelle doubted that he would be able to grasp all of the deep, ancient arts that even she only had a cursory understanding of. Nonetheless, Nelle cast her mind and her spirit outward binding herself further with the complex and powerful connections of nature. The rambling stream. The crumbling rocks. The wisps of plants that clung persistently to life amidst this desolate landscape. The very wind itself. Nelle drew it all into herself and acted as a conduit so that it might flow into Gawain and heal him. What she wouldn't tell Gawain, what she would never tell anyone, was that as she bound herself to these wondrous ancient powers, she also risked completely losing herself.

As she drew another, even more complex and beautiful shape, she saw that her work was nearly complete. The once bloody hole in Gawain's back had closed and was quickly vanishing all together. It was all the to the good, as Nelle wobbled under the effort of it. She felt as if ice ran through her veins and her bones ached from the cold. Yet she forced her fingers to dig into the pocket of her apron and draw out the silver teardrop amulet that she had once offered to Gawain. Hopefully this time he wouldn't be so stubborn and the handsome fool would accept it.

"What is that?" Gawain asked as he offered his face to her, and Nelle began to weave the talisman into his wiry beard.

"Shhh," was her slightly annoyed reply as she forced her fingers to obey and finish the job.

Finally, the tiny silver charm was in place, and Nelle pulled her hands away. Gawain sat up with wide eyes and his mouth hanging agape. He looked like a large stupid child, and Nelle thought about how much she liked him, when a wave of darkness overtook her and she took her turn to fall into unconsciousness.

But the mighty knight caught her in his strong warm arms and held her from the dirt.

"Are you all right?" he asked with worry etched across his already rugged face.

"I'm not a weakling..." she said and she felt a flush of warm pride that she was already awake again. She felt much more resilient than the supposedly legendary knight that now held her so tightly in his comforting arms. She added with her wry mousy smile, "I bet I'm stronger than you…"

"That's how you managed to heal me so quickly back at the castle," he said.

Nelle nodded.

"But I took it slowly then," she explained. "I didn't think you'd go and get yourself shot."

"Your family were more than simple healers, weren't they?" said Gawain, and once again Nelle had the thought that he might not be the brightest, but boy, he sure was nice.

"Witches," she said. "Drawing healing power from the trees and streams. Until the Green Knight came. My father lost a test of strength. And then anyone from my family who dared to fight was killed. Our own power was turned against us. Our healing became the source of our pain."

"And you were forced you to be his slave," said Gawain.

"A spy," Nelle said with a flush of shame and disgust in herself. "I should've been brave like the others, but I agreed to work with the Green Knight. To save myself. I look after those who've fallen under the Green Knight's power. I supposed to help instill fear, and break men's courage. But if I try to use my powers to help anyone, it causes me… well, you can see what it does to me."

"You did the right thing," was Gawain's simple response.

"Now that I've met someone like you, someone so brave, and willing to risk his own life for others, what choice did I have?" said

Nelle with a weak shrug. "Forgive me. I didn't mean to mislead you."

Gawain didn't seem to care at all as he asked, "What did you tell him about me?"

"Just that you're a big monstrous baby," Nelle said with a smile. "Who'll bring an end to this once and for all."

Gawain lifted Nelle up in his arms, and for a brief moment she revelled in the feeling of utter weightlessness that she hadn't enjoyed in years. Gawain settled her into Ringolet's saddle, and then he looked his horse dead in the eye.

"Get her out of here," ordered Gawain. "Take her back to the castle."

"No, I'm fine..." Nelle tried to argue.

Ringolet snuffled indignantly at Gawain. But Gawain glared and even the horse must've known enough to take him seriously.

"It was noble before," he said, "But now, you've got to get the lady to safety."

"I'm not a lady..." Nelle started to protest.

"Yes, you are. Maybe more than any woman I've ever known."

The handsome knight touched her face, then took her small hand in his and kissed it.

"Where will you go?" she dared to ask.

"To bring an end to this," he said. "Once and for all."

Gawain slapped Ringolet on the rump, and the horse dutifully began to climb the back up the rocky ravine. As Nelle clutched to her place in the saddle, she turned back and saw Gawain trudging forward along the narrow stream toward the dark shadowy place that held the Green Knight and probably his doom. Yet his back was straight. His head was held high. His steps never faltered as he bravely marched toward his fate.

All right, yes… Nelle thought, *That's what a real hero looks like.*

~ ~ ~

Sir Bertilak was looking less and less heroic by the second. When that first ferocious bear had stumbled angrily toward the castle, Sir Bertilak had bucked up his courage and thought,

Surely, I can handle just one demonic bear.

Then the bear was joined by a snarling spitting green-eyed fox. Even then he thought,

That's still not too bad, I can handle a bear and fox.

After that a handful of razor-taloned hawks landed on nearby branches.

A bear, a fox, and several hawks. I think, I can do it…

A small army of rats glowing green scuttled out of the forest.

This could be a struggle…

Crows, raccoons, coyotes, and even a badger.

Where are these things coming from?!

When a pack of wolves joined the oncoming horde of beasts, Sir Bertilak finally gave up any hope that he could handle this problem. He had prided himself on his ability to act despite the worst circumstances. He had always believed that no matter what went wrong, if he could just do something, anything, and he would manage to come through it. Now he was paralyzed with fear.

219

Now he couldn't act.

He huddled back toward the castle with the dozens of ragged men, women, and children who had placed their faith in him, who relied on him to do something, anything to help them. Sir Bertilak had nothing but a weak pathetic plea,

"Please... Don't take me... Please... Take Gawain instead..."

~ ~ ~

CHAPTER 19
A Year and a Day

Gawain stomped along the trickle of a stream that had done its best to end him. Now all that it could do was swirl around his feet and make them slightly damp and uncomfortable, but Gawain barely noticed. Up ahead of him was an odd wooden cabin unlike anything he had ever seen before. It was made entirely of thick stacked tree trunks. The roof met with tall, crisscrossing beams. In and of itself, none of that was strange, but what was unnerving was that the entire structure was covered in thick heavy green moss and snaking creeping vines. The choking plants gave the place an otherworldly green hue that almost glowed amongst the dark shadows cast by the mountains that stood on either side of it. Nonetheless, Gawain ventured straight for it without even breaking his stride.

He reached the twenty foot tall wooden doors and grabbed hold of a large handle carved in the beams. Gawain had to use all his strength and lurch back with all his weight just to get the doors to budge, and he was reminded, with a tingle of fear, how easily the Green Knight had opened the massive ornate doors in Uther Pendragon's feasting halls. Inch by creaking inch, Gawain forced open the doors to the strange green chapel, until there was finally a gap large enough for him to squeeze through.

221

The inside of the place was even stranger still. It was a cavernous hunter's lodge to put all others to shame. Heads of deer, moose, horse and reindeer lined the walls. Stuffed eagles, hawks and owls were arranged with their wings spread wide as if they were preparing to take off at any moment. The bodies of carefully posed bears, wolves and lions were stationed alongside even stranger creatures like a sphinx, a griffin and even a curled-up, hundred foot long basilisk. Most unsettling of all were suits of armor standing in the corners with, Gawain realized with an entirely unmanly gasp of terror, their owners still imprisoned forever inside.

And at the far back wall there was a tall wooden throne where sat the Green Knight himself, eagerly watching the arrival of Sir Gawain.

"Ah, Sir Gawain!" boomed the Green Knight genially. "I am most impressed to see you here!"

"We had an appointment, I believe," grumbled Gawain.

"You might be surprised how precious few people show up for their appointments," beamed the Green Knight in his frustratingly polite manner.

"Clearly I'm a lot less intelligent than most people," said Gawain, then added with a shrug, "But a lot more ruggedly handsome."

"You truly are a man of honor."

The Green Knight rose out of his throne and, without delay, he drew the massive double-headed ax from off of his back as he strode toward Gawain.

"Shall we then?"

"Wait," said Gawain and he was relieved to see that the Green Knight paused expectantly, "I have a request of you."

"I am always willing to listen, my good knight," said the Green Knight.

"I'm here to square our deal," said Gawain. "But I ask you to please add one more to it. Spare Sir Bertilak's lands and his people."

"And Sir Bertilak himself?" asked the Green Knight with a knowing smile.

Gawain waffled then shrugged as he let out a deep sigh.

"Him too. The great scheming git."

"But what do I get out of it?" wondered the Green Knight.

Gawain fell silent for a moment. Since he woke up that morning, he had been preparing for this. In fact, he'd been preparing for it for a year now. Maybe even his entire life. Up until this point he'd always been ruled by pride. He accepted adventures and crusades if he felt they would help lend a mythic air to the legend he so sought to create. But he realized, with more than a twinge of guilt, that it had almost always been primarily for his own glory. Certainly, he had helped hundreds, if not thousands of people, but that was always a side benefit. Everything he had done, he had done to make himself greater. However, now he stood alone with the Green Knight in a distant green chapel hidden in the shadow of two mountains in deserted, wretched Old Swythamley. No one would know what he did here today. It had no chance of being discovered and added to his legend. Yet it was the right thing to do, and Gawain knew it.

He flipped his sword and proffered the hilt to the massive emerald man standing before him.

"I'll let you strike me down undefended," said Gawain. "I won't put up a fight at all."

"And why should I be interested in that?" asked the Green Knight.

"Because you're worried I might beat you," said Gawain and he could tell by the shocked expression on the Green Knight's normally implacable face that he was right. "As far as I can tell, no one's ever shown up for their rematch. You've gone to great lengths to scare them all away. But you wouldn't go through all that trouble if you knew you were always bound to win. You can be beaten. And you know if anyone would be able to do it, it's me."

For once, the Green Knight seemed uncharacteristically speechless. Gawain took one moment to embrace his small victory before he continued.

"Yet I'm willing to give it all up," said Gawain as he offered his sword once more. "If you'll agree to spare the people of Hautdesert Castle as well as my people in Tintagel."

"You truly are an exceptional knight, Sir Gawain," said the Green Knight as he strode forward and took hold of the hilt of Gawain's sword. Gawain gave no resistance as the blade slid from his hand. "But can you truly be this courageous? This bold? This proud?"

"I'm not proud at all for the things I've done," admitted Gawain. "Go ahead. Strike."

And the Green Knight did.

With all his massive strength, the towering emerald knight drove the sword all the way through Gawain. The force of the blow hit Gawain like the charge of a bull, but he was pleased with himself for being able to stay on his feet. At least for a moment. Then the strength gave out of mighty Sir Gawain legs, his knees buckled and collapsed to the ground.

The Green Knight clapped as he declared, "Truly a thrilling display. Truly thrilling."

Then, leaving his foe crumbled and utterly defeated on the floor, the Green Knight stepped casually over Gawain's body and headed for the door.

"Wait…" gasped Gawain as the sword through his middle restricted his ability to draw a full breath, yet he managed to utter, "Where… where are you going…?"

"To conquer Sir Bertilak and his lands, of course," said the Green Knight as if it was the most obvious thing in the world. Then he added just as plainly, "And then yours."

"We had… an agreement…," growled Gawain as his vision blurred around the edges.

"I don't keep agreements with dead men," said the Green Knight. "You need to stop being so trusting, Sir Gawain."

And with that, the Green Knight dissolved into green mist and vanished just as Sir Gawain gasped his last breath and expired.

~ ~ ~

The madness outside of Hautdesert Castle had reached a furious, horrifying, hopeless peak. Ferocious green-eyed beasts swarmed and snarled and spat. And the meager group of people could do little to slow them down.

Nonetheless, Sir Bertilak urged them on as he shouted, "Fight! Every last man, woman, and child! Take up arms! Push them back."

However, his words had completely lost their ability to inspire or to instill confidence in the terrified masses. The lord of Hautdesert Castle was sounding more and more crazed, at one point he had even suggested that they "aim for the ears! They won't expect that!"

The fight was hopeless even without the ineffectual leadership of Sir Bertilak. All around the frightened people were being struck and beaten by the horde of beasts. A massive roaring bear lumbered forward and swiped its merciless paws at an old man who crumpled a the vicious blow. A group of women with their meager brooms tried to fend off a pack of foaming foxes, but it did little good. A hawk swooped down from the black skies and slashed its razor-sharp talons along the arm of a small boy. Screams and shrieks of pain filled the night air along with the roars and squeals of the unnatural beasts.

"What are you scared of?" came Sir Bertilak's battle cry. "Fight! Fight! We can win!"

But the battle was moving in the wrong direction. Slowly, the small group of survivors were being forced back against the castle walls. They had that meager safety at their backs, but it wouldn't spare them for long. They needed a real leader. They needed a real voice of reason. They needed a miracle.

Which was exactly what they got as a gray speckled horse galloped out of the woods and threw itself into the fray.

For a glorious moment, all of the gathered beasts fell back at the stomping of the horse. Many of the women wept that the sight, and they barely registered as Nelle, the tiny nurse that they hadn't even realized was missing all this time, slipped off of the horse's back. She quickly made her presence known as she shouted with a voice stronger than any of them had heard her use before.

"Everyone... follow me!" she said firmly even though it appeared that it was costing her all of her strength just to stand up straight. "We have to barricade ourselves in the dungeon..."

As the horse sprung and stamped at the army of beasts, the word spread amongst the people that were gathered there and they followed the nurse. Nelle led them all along the castle wall until they reached an oak door. Nelle grabbed ahold of the brass handle and tried to wrench it open. But she didn't have the strength. In fact, she nearly collapsed under the effort of all she had done so far.

"What are you doing?" demanded Sir Bertilak. "We can't give up! We can still save our lands!"

But no one was willing to follow him anymore. Instead, several of the other servants jumped to the aid of Nelle. In a moment, they had wrenched the dungeon door open, and one-by-by the nurse ushered each of the frightened people inside, all the while insisting that she would be last.

The beasts had recovered from their initial shock at the galloping horse and they were now regaining their boldness as they nipped and bit at the outmatched horse. With a final burst of a energy, the horse lunged at a wolf and it fell back. Then, the horse turned to Nelle and offered its head to her. She patted it appreciatively on the neck

"You've done all you can here, Ringolet…" said the small grateful nurse to the impossibly brave horse. "Now go… Get out of here… Live a long horse life."

And the mighty horse galloped off into the night, just as the last of the servants, men, women, and children rushed into the dungeon. Nelle headed for the door herself, but as she reached for the handle, another hand grabbed it at the same time. Sir Bertilak was still hoping to save his own neck by barricading himself in with the others, and possibly even offering them up in place of himself.

But Nelle still had enough strength to shove the cowardly lord out of the way.

"You've got to let me in too!" cried Sir Bertilak.

Even as he said it, though, they turned to watch as a thick green mist floated in on the gray colorless air. The mist settled into the vague shape of a man before solidifying into a towering brute of an emerald knight.

"I think you still have an appointment," said Nelle as she ducked into the dungeon and pulled the door shut behind her.

Sir Bertilak turned to face the now fully materialized Green Knight, and the once proud lord fell to his knees.

"Ah, the brave and righteous Sir Bertilak! It is time to pay your debt, my friend!" said the Green Knight.

"Please... End this..." pleaded Sir Bertilak miserably. "I gave you Sir Gawain! Wasn't that enough?!"

~ ~ ~

CHAPTER 20

The Green Sash

Gawain was dead.

At least he thought he was.

How else could he explain the lack of pain? Why else would he feel so restful? What else could be the reason that he finally felt calm and warm and almost peaceful?

And yet he couldn't deny that his nose was a little itchy.

After a few confused moments, Gawain opened his eyes. He could still open his eyes. He twitched his arms and legs. His arms and legs still worked. He rose into a sitting position despite the fact that he still had a sword through him. With an expectation of blinding pain that never came, Gawain gripped the hilt of his sword and drew it out of his belly. He tossed it aside. He grumbled. He could still grumble.

Finally scratching his nose, Gawain got to his feet and tried to make sense of this most strange development. And as he dragged his fingernails roughly along the length of his nose and satisfied his annoying itch, Gawain bumped the heel of his hand against something.

The teardrop shaped silver amulet.

After a moment of confusion, Gawain pulled it out of his beard and cracked it open. With a yelp of a laugh, Gawain found the green sash crumbled inside into the tiniest of balls. Gawain unfurled it and it stretched out almost impossible long despite its tiny enclosure like a magician pulling out a handkerchief from his glove.

"How did she get ahold of it?" he wondered aloud, but the answer dawned upon him almost as soon as he said it. "The stables. She could pick up all sorts of treasures."

There was no more time to marvel over it, Gawain had work to do. Once again, Nelle had saved him. She had given him a gift. And he was determined to repay the favor. Not only that, but he was dying to get his hands on that duplicitous cheating Green Knight. The familiar thrill of adventure flooded through Gawain as he charged for the door. But before he was able to reach it,

BAM!

The doors to the green chapel burst open and Ringolet galloped in.

"What took you so long?!"

Ringolet huffed at his master. But without a moment's hesitation, Gawain mounted and together they headed off to finally bring an end to their adventure.

~ ~ ~

The Green Knight gazed down at the pitiful man at his feet. The once proud Sir Bertilak, who had boasted endlessly of his skill with a bow and his ability to send a perfect volley into the heart of any beast, was now thoroughly beaten. A horde of beasts was at the

231

ready just behind the Green Knight, and they were positively salivating at the chance to get their teeth into the fallen lord.

"Please…" sobbed Sir Bertilak. "Please… let it be over… just end this…"

"But you brought this upon yourself, my poor friend," said the Green Knight. "Men like you, full of pride but ultimately cowardice, always bring these fates upon themselves."

"You've taken my lands! Killed my people! Destroyed my castle! Haven't you taken enough?!" cried Sir Bertilak.

"Ah, but that wasn't our deal, my good sir," said the Green Knight. "You were only too happy to place the safety of your people and your lands on the line for the chance to proudly show off your skill. You were so certain that you couldn't be beaten that you ignored the cost. But you lost and now there is a debt to be paid. I intend to collect."

Sir Bertilak sagged even further into despair knowing that all hope was lost. He couldn't even bring himself to look into the face of the towering green man any longer. The Green Knight took his massive double-headed ax into his hands and felt its terrible weight. These were the delicious moments that he couldn't savor long enough. He raised the killing weapon high into the air.

"Please… please… I tried…"

SWOOSH!

Sir Bertilak's body crumbled. Dead. But the deal still wasn't settled. There was payment yet to be made. With a grin, the Green Knight raised his hand and urged his horde of beasts forward. The bears, wolves, foxes, hawks, rats, and all manner of monster rushed forward upon the castle's walls. They converged on the lone protection left to the people of Hautdesert Castle. A simple wooden door between the Green Knight and the dungeon. The beasts pounded at the wood, scratched at the ground, and clawed at the stone walls.

It wouldn't be long now.

~   ~   ~

Down in the depths of the dungeon, the terrible sounds of the beasts echoed along the stone stairwell and were magnified to a horrifying degree in the cavernous room. Everyone huddled together as they listened to the pounding, the howling, the clawing.

Everyone except for Nelle.

She couldn't blame people for being frightened. But she also knew that cowering in fear was going to do very little for them now. She was determined to stay strong, and she would do all she could to keep everyone else strong for however many moments might be left to them.

"We'll be all right... We'll make it through this..." she said with all the volume she could muster into her voice. "Now... Who's hurt?"

No one said a word or even made the slightest move to show that they had heard her. Clearly she'd have to do more.

"Come now!" she shouted and caused several of the children to stop crying from surprise at her outburst. "We've just been through a battle! There's no need for anyone else to die down here! Now, who's hurt?"

After a long shocked moment, an old man that Nelle recognized as one of the groundskeepers shuffled forward. In the old man's arms was a young boy, and streaking down the boy's arm were three long red slashes. The boy had been clawed by a hawk. But, although he was shaking with fear and pain, the boy was still alive, and as the old man presented the child to Nelle, the nurse determined to keep him that way.

Nelle gritted her jaw and focused all of her heat into her hands. She could barely breath, she could barely see, she could barely hold herself up. But she wasn't going to give in that easily. She was going to be brave like Sir Gawain. She was going to pay for the sins that she had committed in service to the Green Knight.

As the rattling madness outside echoed down into the dungeon, Nelle placed her hands on the boy's wounds and she felt the warmth pour into him. And she felt the cold tearing at her.

~ ~ ~

CHAPTER 21

The Final Rematch

The animals ripped at the dungeon door with their claws, talons and teeth. As one spitting foaming mass they attacked the door into the castle and it seemed destined to fall away any moment now.

Pound, rip, scratch, tear...

The door buckled.

Pound, rip, scratch, tear...

It splintered and cracked.

Pound, rip, scratch, tear...

It was about to break apart.

BOOM!

All of the animals spun as the light of a bright blazing flame roared behind them. The Green Knight and his horde of animals all turned to see Sir Gawain standing beside Ringolet. A tall bonfire blazed and lit up the profiles of the great man and his horse. Forgetting about the all-too-feeble door, the horde of beast turned their attention to this new feast that lay before them for the taking.

But Gawain had no intention of dying again today.

"Ready to die, my friend?" asked the knight to his horse.

The horse shook his head.

"Neither am I," grinned Gawain. "I suppose, we'll just have to slay every last one of them instead."

Ringolet nodded. And neighed. Gawain had always had a good understanding of a what Ringolet meant to communicate, and he was pretty sure that right now the horse was saying,

Let's go to war.

But the Green Knight confidently strode forward with the beasts snarling at his heels.

"Ah, the mighty Sir Gawain returns," he said. "It seems you have many tricks up your sleeve, my friend. And here I thought you were an honest man."

"I wouldn't speak of honesty if I were you," growled Gawain. "You miserable, sneaking coward."

"Coward? I'm not the one who needs my back to a fire," said the Green Knight.

"It seems to be the only sure way to keep you and your beasts at bay," said Gawain and then he added, "You're not a fan of fire, are you? That's why there were no torches in your chapel. It's why your beasts could never attack at night. And it's why you wouldn't light that torch against the wolves."

The Green Knight looked bemused but inclined his head slightly as he urged Gawain to go on. Gawain was happy to continue. There had always been things about Hautdesert Castle that hadn't rung true to Gawain. There were small inconsistencies, little doubts that continually nagged at his mind. Having a sword driven through his gut had given Gawain surprising clarity about it all. He felt certain that he knew the true nature of the Green Knight, and now was the time to test his deadly foe and find out what he was really up against.

"That's why you're the Wind Lady. Isn't that right, Lady Bertilak?" said Gawain.

The Green Knight grinned, "Well done, Sir Gawain. Well done!"

His towering seven foot form dissolved into green mist momentarily and then reformed itself into the visage of Lady Bertilak. However, she was different from the lady that Gawain had experienced up until that point. Now she glowed emerald green just like the armored knight that had haunted Gawain's dreams. And she was still dressed in that green armor although it had shrunk to fit her seemingly delicate form. However, in her hands was still the massive double-headed ax, and Lady Bertilak seemed still able to wield it with ease. Gawain guessed that she wasn't nearly as delicate as she seemed.

"I'm impressed, Sir Gawain," said the green glowing lady. "How long have you known?"

"There's been something strange about you from the beginning," admitted Gawain. "But it all comes down to the fact that you would've said and done anything to keep me away from my rematch. Just like you did with your husband."

"Ah, but that's the true test of pride," she said in the same genial manner as she had in her guise as the Green Knight. "It's not merely the battle and the rematch. It's the build-up, the anticipation.

237

The fight against fear. It's keeping your word even when it means certain doom."

"Shall we finally have our rematch then?" asked Gawain.

"Soon, I think. But not yet. Because now you have a secret..." she said. "Tell me, Sir Gawain, how did you survive back in my chapel?"

Gawain drew out the green sash from his belt.

"Nelle," Lady Bertilak said as she shook her head and her long blonde hair swayed at her sides. "And she had always been such a good servant. She'll have to be dealt with now."

"Only if you walk away from here," Gawain said.

With that, Gawain tossed the green sash into the fire. It flared and was consumed in moments. Now there were no more tricks. No more guises. No more deceptions. There was only Gawain and his green foe. They were finally at the end.

"This time I fully intend to fight," he said. "Without any protections. Just you and I. Once and for all. For these lands and for my own. I'll put an end to your villainy."

Lady Bertilak smiled as she took a step closer to Gawain. Then with astonishing speed and force she reared back and punched Gawain in the chest. Gawain had taken many punches over his storied career. He had even taken more than his share over the course of the last year. One thing that he had always learned was that the first punch was more shocking than painful. He could always take the first punch reasonably well. It was the second, third, fourth and so on that started to take their toll. This time, however, as he was sent careening through the air by the first brutal swing, Gawain had to admit that it hurt. A lot. He was in for the fight of his life.

"I'm really frightened..." Lady Bertilak said without the slightest hint of fear.

~ ~ ~

Nelle pulled her hands off of a maid's leg. The woman's skin was bare, unblemished and remarkably healed. But Nelle wasn't not looking so good. Every move had become an effort. Every breath was a struggle. Darkness kept crowding into the edges of her vision, and Nelle had to keep blinking to clear her mind. She had given more of herself than she had imagined she could, but there were still more wounded men, women, and children. She had a vague understanding that somewhere deep inside, she'd passed a point of no return. The healing arts that she called upon had taken an immense toll, and she'd never be able to come back completely from the work she was doing. Yet, she had no intention of stopping now as she asked,

"Who's... next...?"

~ ~ ~

Gawain and Lady Bertilak were locked into a battle that would make any knight swell with pride. As he barely managed to avoid a swing of her double-headed ax, Gawain had to admit that he was outmatched by Lady Bertilak's unnatural strength and speed. But he hadn't become the greatest knight in the land by being the best with the sword or the strongest of strong men. He had become the best by one simple trick.

He just kept getting up.

No matter how many times Lady Bertilak knocked him down, Gawain had decided this time, once and for all, he'd keep getting up until she could no longer get up herself. He took a mighty swipe at her with his broadsword, but she met it with a strike of her ax. The impact caused Gawain to crash painfully backward into the ground.

But he got up.

In the blink of an eye, Lady Bertilak had closed the distance, and she kicked Gawain hard to the ribs. As he fell, he felt at least one of his ribs break from the impact.

But he got up.

Lady Bertilak swung the butt of her ax and caught Gawain under the chin. The world became a blur of confusing colors, as Gawain flipped end over end before slamming back to the frozen earth.

But he got up.

As Gawain struggled to his feet, forcing his eyes to focus as he continued the fight, a snarling wolf pounced at him. Gawain spun and tried to brace himself, but he knew he was going to take a hit. And it was going to hurt. Fortunately, Gawain had something else on his side.

A loyal horse.

Ringolet charged forward and threw all of his weight toward the foaming wolf. The green-eyed beast fell back. Gawain watched as Ringolet continued his charge, circling around the fire, keeping the other animals at bay, and giving Gawain the space to continue his duel.

Using the freedom, Gawain slashed at Lady Bertilak once more. But almost too easily, she caught the blade with her free hand, its cutting edge leaving no effect upon her.

"I will give you credit, Sir Gawain, you're the strongest man I've yet destroyed," she said. "But take my word, I will most assuredly still destroy you."

"I take that as a compliment," groaned Gawain as he struggled against her surprising strength. "I've seen much of your handiwork."

"It's been a pleasure bringing foolish proud men like you to their knees," she said.

She twisted the blade and her leverage forced Gawain down to his knees. A bear lumbered forward to strike at Gawain. But just as quickly, Ringolet darted to the rescue and kicked the bear with his hind legs. The bear tumbled into the fire, roared in pain, then dissolved into a green mist as it was consumed by the flames.

"You won't have many servants left soon," said Gawain as he threw all his weight into Lady Bertilak hoping to budge her toward the fire.

However, Lady Bertilak simply used Gawain's own momentum to lift him improbably high into the air. She flipped him, and although Gawain managed to land on his feet, it was now his back to the fire. And it was Lady Bertilak turn to push.

"Oh, I don't need any servants. Just me."

Gawain struggled with all his might, but his feet couldn't maintain a purchase on the dirt. Inch by inch he slipped backward toward the flames. Lady Bertilak smiled as she tossed her flowing dirty blonde hair over her shoulder, and forced Gawain ever closer to his fiery demise.

"Can't you see!?" she said. "You brought this destruction upon yourself and those you care about. You are the King of the Fire. Smiting all that come in contact with you. I'm merely the wind lady. Feeding the flames within you."

"No! I'm a good man," he said, trying desperately to find a way to stop her terrible push, but only slipping closer to the fire.

"No, no, no. You're a disaster. You're a disrupter. You make everything worse."

The flames of the bonfire tickled at Gawain's back, and he growled with pain. He couldn't hope to beat her in a show of strength. No matter what he did, he seemed sure to end up in the fire.

So he decided he might as well have it be on his own terms.

"Well, if I'm the King of the Fire, then let me embrace the flames!" he roared.

And then he grabbed Lady Bertilak in a bear hug. With all of his strength, Gawain squeezed Lady Bertilak tightly against him. They became like one tangled massive. They almost could have been lovers if not for the screams of fury that erupted from each of them. Then Gawain arched his back and lifted the lady just a few inches from the ground. He squatted, wrenched his body, then leapt backward, thrusting them both through the massive flames. The heat engulfed him and the flames tickled at him, roasting his skin and singing hair.On all sides of them, the fire embraced them, and it attacked every bare bit of flesh on his face, hands and torso.

They emerged on the other side of the fire, both smoking and cindering, and they slammed to the ground together. Gawain's skin screamed from the intensity of the burn, but he could quickly tell that it had taken much more of a toll on Lady Bertilak. The green lady writhed in pain, but Gawain had a feeling that it wouldn't last long. In the quick instant of weakness, Gawain grabbed his sword and leapt at the lady. She was pulling herself together and the rage in her eyes blazed like the fire that they had just passed through. But it was too late for her, and Gawain stabbed his broadsword through her belly, feeling a flush of pleasure at striking her in much the same way she had so recently struck him. She shrieked in pain, and Gawain was pleased to see that at the same moment, all of the beasts that did her bidding had also fallen and were writhing in similar pain and anguish.

"I know you could just pull that out," said Gawain. "But it should slow you down long enough for me to put you in the fire where you belong."

The mighty knight lifted the evil lady up into the air. He walked the few short steps toward the fire and was about to throw her in, when her cold voice brought him up short.

"You think you've won...?" she gasped. "No... Uther Pendragon and young Arthur still aren't safe."

Gawain lurched in surprise, "What do they have to do with this?"

"They were always my eventual goal," she said with a grin of savage pleasure. "All the others were just practice. My Queen's been dying to get at Uther and the boy."

"Your Queen?"

"The Queen of the Feys," said Lady Bertilak. "I was only a simple woman with a simple talent for destroying the simple men who bothered me. Until she gave me real power. Then I was able to bring the most powerful of men to their knees. I made castles crumble. I bent nature itself to my will. And it was all thanks to her. When she comes for you, and mark my words, she will most certainly come for you, she'll make you wish I'd killed you."

"Let her come! I'll slay her just like I've slain you and all of your servants!"

Gawain reared back and was about to throw Lady Bertilak in the fire and be done with it, but it turned out that she had one last surprise.

"*All* of my servants?!"

Gawain paused at her strange taunt and almost immediately his eyes locked on the dungeon door. His heart fell. An old man emerged from the depths of the castle, and in his aging but strong arms he carried Nelle. But the tiny nurse was writhing in pain. Just like Lady Bertilak. Just like the beasts. Just like all who served the power of the Green Knight.

"No!" shouted Gawain and the sight of the poor sweet nurse twisting in agony caused the mighty knight more pain than any mere sword ever could.

"Did you think this would be easy, Sir Gawain?" whispered Lady Bertilak. "Doing the right thing seldom is…"

Across the fire, Gawain locked eyes with Nelle. Tears rolled down her tender face, but she seemed determined as she mouthed her final request to Gawain.

"Do it… Finish this…" gasped Nelle.

Gawain gripped Lady Bertilak tighter. He cocked his arms back to throw her. But he couldn't do it. He roared in frustration as tears began to stream down his face.

"Could you ever be proud of yourself again?" asked Lady Bertilak.

"It's all right… End it…" said Nelle through her gasps of pain.

"Can you really let that poor girl die?"

"Please… I forgive you…"

"She's so much better than you."

"Gawain… do the right thing…"

Finally, even though it took every ounce of strength he had, Gawain tossed Lady Bertilak into the fire. The beautiful blonde lady screamed as the immense heat engulfed her. In mere moments, she dissolved into a burst of green and was consumed by the flames. All around Gawain the bears, wolves, foxes, hawks and beasts writhed and also began to fade away into quickly vanishing bursts of green mist, but the knight paid them no heed.

Gawain raced over to Nelle's side. He took the her from the old man and Gawain held the nurse in his arms as she slowly began to fade away into faint green nothingness.

"I'm so so sorry," he said and unbidden tears were already pouring down his cheeks and flooding into his beard.

"You did what had to be done... You should be proud..." she sighed.

"I don't know if I can ever be proud again."

Nelle lifted herself close enough to be face-to-face with Gawain. She pressed her soft lips against his, and as he accepted the kiss, he knew that he would never have another like it for as long as he lived.

"Of course you can. After all, you did the right thing," she said tenderly before adding, "You big, whimpering, sobbing baby."

She smiled at him. That mousy wry beautiful smile. And then her smile faded away along with the rest of her as she vanished into the green mist and was lost to the gently blowing wind.

Gawain crumbled.

Whimpering and sobbing.

Like a baby.

~   ~   ~

As the night stretched on and sunrise approached, a light snowfall began to dance upon the soft chill breeze. At first the few meager flakes were quickly consumed by the massive bonfire that still burned brightly in the feasting circle. But slowly as the snow fell steadier and more heavily, the winter storm began to overcome the raging fire. Inch by inch the flames fell back, and their orange and yellow fingers failed to tickle the sky any longer. Slowly, the outer edges of the fire died away. Then the wood that had been furthest from the center sizzled and cooled. Thick gray clouds of smoke began to waft away from the quickly dying fire as the unceasing onslaught of snow fell. The fire shrank slowly but steadily until the strengthening snowfall finally extinguished the last of its dying embers and the world became quiet.

And Gawain knelt upon the freezing ground and sobbed.

The snow had piled into his hair and beard and tiny icicles were beginning to form. He had long since run out of tears, but melting snowflakes merged into small streams as they ran down his reddening frozen cheeks. The snow began to pile up around his knees. His fingers and toes began to ache from the cold. But Gawain didn't care. He was exhausted, broken, and simply wished for the snow to pile up so high that it would overcome him like a clean white blanket that could grant him a sleep that he might never awaken from.

But then his friend came to his side.

Ringolet's hooves left faint tracks in the soft layer of snow as he approached Gawain. The horse bent its long head and gently licked the ice off of the freezing face of his master, and he chewed the icicles off of Gawain's snow encrusted beard. After a long battle with his own stubborness, Gawain raised his head. Ringolet nuzzled against his master's great beard, and Gawain patted Ringolet's soft mane.

Slowly, Gawain rose to his feet and as he did, he realized that he wasn't alone. He turned to see that a small group of people was beginning to emerge from the dungeon. The ragged men, women and children had come through the battle, but now they looked to Gawain for guidance on where to go next.

But he had never felt more lost himself.

"I'd bring you all back if I could, but we'd never make the journey," he said and he could see by the looks on their faces that they agreed. "But the danger's past now. You can rebuild here."

Then as Gawain's thoughts returned to Nelle, he added softly, "And you'll be safer without me anyway."

Finally Gawain turned to Ringolet and mounted onto the horse's back.

"Come on, old friend," said the wounded knight to his sturdy horse. "It's time to go home."

And together they rode toward the softly cresting horizon.

~ ~ ~

EPILOGUE

Gawain's Legacy

"With hearts full of sadness,
They rode on for their homes,
They took many months
Their exploits could fill tomes.
But onward they rode south
Kept steady their course.
And return'd home victorious
Sir Gawain and his Great Horse."

As the morning sun rose and the small crackling campfire died away, Arthur finished his tale and fell silent. The young king bowed his golden head in silent remembrance of his friend and mentor. But then a smirk crossed his face.

Gawain had always been a good storyteller.

Even in the last few months of his life, after he had returned from his crusade against the Green Knight, Gawain had liked to boast of his many travels and adventures. True, he had come back from Hautdesert Castle a changed man, and wasn't nearly the light-hearted, boisterous warrior that he had been when he left, but Gawain was always warm, always generous, and always entertaining. Arthur was fairly certain that Gawain would've been pleased to know that his story was being used to train a new generation of brave and noble knights.

For their part, the half dozen knights-in-training gave a small, somewhat subdued round of applause for their king's story. Arthur looked around and saw that each of the young men was now able to move their arms quite freely, their eyes looked clear, and a few of them were even bold enough to try and stand up again, which they did successfully, although they might have wobbled just a bit. Arthur shot a glance over at Guinevere and they both nodded to each other. Their training ruse seemed to have been effective, and the diluted basilik venom seemed to have passed through the knights-in-training with no lasting effects.

Overall, not a bad endeavour.

"Here, here!" a few of the knights-in-training called to Arthur. A few others variously threw in their appreciative comments of, "Well done!" or "Huzzah!"

"Well, it seems as if your voices have returned," said Arthur as he rose to his feet and stretched his legs. "And I think you should all be able to walk again."

As Arthur stood up straight all of his subjects did the same. One or two of them shuddered precariously and seemed to be on the verge of toppling over, but they managed to right themselves. With a look that was maybe a bit too expectant to be really kind, Guinevere watched one of the knights-in-training nearly collapse, but he wrenched himself straight at the last moment. Guinevere actually seemed disappointed. Arthur had to laugh, his lady had always liked a good show.

"Let us start the long journey back," said Arthur.

With that, Arthur stamped out the final embers of the dying campfire. A few of the young men began to journey into the surrounding woods, and Arthur was once again assured that he had chosen them all well as he watched them confidently striking off toward the north in search of the newly built castle that they all called home. First they would reunite with the other knights that were being led by Sir Percival. Then they would all begin the long trek back. It would take several days to make the return, but Arthur knew that every journey began with a single step, and he took it, and he was off to his kingdom.

"Sir, King Arthur, sir...?" the clean-cut knight-in-training stammered as he approached. Once again Arthur had to marvel at the young man who was by far the most brave and capable in battle yet seemed so nervous in addressing his king. But then Arthur reminded himself that he was, in fact, the king and that could be a very intimidating thing.

"Arthur is fine," said Arthur, and he cast Guinevere a quick smile as he added, "We don't have much use for titles."

"What happened to the Queen of the Feys?" asked the young man. "Did Gawain ever hear anything more about her?"

"No," admitted Arthur. "He remained on the look out for her, of course, but she never reappeared. And we've had quite enough enemies to keep busy with as it is."

"When we get back, I'll look into this Queen of the Feys," said the knight-in-training decisively. "It only makes sense to be prepared."

"I'm sure Gawain would feel in your debt," said Arthur.

"I-I knew Sir Gawain, sir, Arthur, sir," said the young man hesitantly, as if he wasn't sure it was something he should reveal to his king. "I was only a young boy when I saw him. But he left quite an impression on me. He was the one who made me want to become a knight."

A flash of comprehension hit Arthur and suddenly it all made sense. The skills in battle. The knowledge of that particular blow to the sternum. The determined insistence to do right.

"That's how you knew the move so well..." marvelled Arthur. "You were the boy being picked on in Sir Gawain's story."

"No," said the clean-cut young man, and as his gaze fell it was tough to tell in the dim light, but Arthur suspected he was blushing with shame. "No, you see, I had the move used on me. I was one of the bullies. I'm not proud of it."

"What's your name, my friend?" asked Arthur.

"Tristam, sir."

"I suspect that very soon you'll be the one we call 'Sir'," said Arthur as he patted Tristam on the shoulder.

Tristam flushed again and Arthur was pleased to see that the young man hadn't let the compliment fill him with an over abundance of pride like it might lesser men. In fact, Arthur realized that for this young man, shame was actually a much stronger

252

motivator than pride. There were always new lessons to be learned, and Arthur wondered if one day he might be using the story of Tristam to teach about some other virtue. Or vice. With those thoughts churning in his mind, Arthur watched as young Tristam rushed ahead and caught up with the other men.

Suddenly, a soft yet firm hand slipped into Arthur's and intertwined its fingers with his. Guinevere stepped up beside Arthur and with natural ease they quickly fell into step with one another. Arthur always felt in such easy rhythm with Guinevere, and he hoped that, despite whatever challenges and adventures lay ahead for him, that was one thing that would never change.

"I do love your stories," she said.

"What's not to like?" asked Arthur with a good-natured shrug. "Adventure, humor, romance."

"Tragedy," added Guinevere. "I noticed you gave this one a somewhat happier ending. I'm not quite sure that's how Gawain would've told it."

"No. I suspect he would not have…" agreed Arthur with a grave note to his voice and once again his mind flooded and churned with thoughts and images. He saw his great friend, Sir Gawain, and his terrible return to Tintagel.

"Tell me the real ending," Guinevere said.

For a few strides, Arthur slowed his pace and Guinevere matched him appropriately. They fell back a few steps from the young men who were marching boldly toward their destiny. For the moment, Arthur wanted them to focus on the great potential that the future held for them. They would each have the chance to save lives, to win love, and to experience happiness. Arthur wanted to instill that hope and excitement into each of them for now. There would be another time for them to learn the other lessons that Gawain's example could teach. Eventually they would learn about disappointment and heartbreak and loss. However, for the moment, Arthur kept the rest of the story for himself and Guinevere. The young king pictured his friend, Gawain, riding up to Tintagel Castle with his face full of sadness. Yet the tired warrior's heart was full of hope for a castle waiting for him with open arms of friendship. Instead, he found Tintagel smoldering, destroyed, and conquered with a Red Dragon perched upon its walls, and King Uther Pendragon dead and defeated.

Arthur cleared his throat and spoke in a clear whisper that only Guinevere could hear as he finished the tale,

"They return'd home victorious
Sir Gawain and his horse.
But when they returned home,
They despised what they saw.
It stole way his strong speech
And it filled him awe.
The kingdom was taken
By a beast with fire breath,
And gone was the good king,
Brought down to his death.
He had hoped to return
To the bed where he slept.

254

But Gawain he fell down

To the ground and he wept."

~ ~ ~

THE END

~ ~ ~

For more of

THE LEGENDS OF KING ARTHUR

look for these installments:

~ ~ ~

AUTHOR'S BIO

Ben Gillman is an L.A.-based novelist and screenwriter. He's been a fan of Arthurian legend ever since "First Knight" (starring Sean Connery as King Arthur) became the first movie he ever saw twice in the theatres. In college he studied English Literature and immersed himself in Arthurian legends as told by Thomas Mallory and T.H. White. Now he's the writer of dozens of action-adventure novels and films, as well as many comedic sketches and plays. He lives with his wife, Vered, in Southern California.

Made in the USA
Columbia, SC
04 April 2019